Now.. P9-EGL-551

Harlequin

romance
by Anne Mather
comes to life
on the movie screen

starring

KEIR DULLEA · SUSAN PENHALIGON

Leopard in the Snow

Guest Stars
KENNETH MORE · BILLIE WHITELAW

featuring GORDON THOMSON as MICHAEL
and JEREMY KEMP as BOLT

Produced by JOHN QUESTED and CHRIS HARROP
Screenplay by ANNE MATHER and JILL HYEM
Directed by GERRY O'HARA

An Anglo-Canadian Co-Production

OTHER
Harlequin Romances
by MARGARET ROME

Many of these titles are available at your local bookseller,
or through the Harlequin Reader Service.

For a free catalogue listing all available Harlequin Romances,
send your name and address to:

HARLEQUIN READER SERVICE,
M.P.O. Box 707, Niagara Falls, N.Y. 14302
Canadian address: Stratford, Ontario, Canada N5A 6W4

or use order coupon at back of books.

Lion
of Venice

by

MARGARET ROME

Harlequin Books

TORONTO • LONDON • NEW YORK • AMSTERDAM • SYDNEY

Original hardcover edition published in 1977
by Mills & Boon Limited

ISBN 0-373-02152-6

Harlequin edition published March 1978

CHAPTER ONE

'Jo, if you don't make up your mind to marry soon I swear I'll retreat into a convent, or fade into a decline or ... or——'

'Take up acting as a profession? Really, Sara, whosoever it was that stated: "All the world's a stage" must have had someone very much like yourself in mind!'

Sara's pleading pout hardened into a grimace as she directed a look of dislike towards her elder sister. 'Papà always said you ought to have been a boy, but however hard you try you'll never make up to him for the son he never had.' She was too lacking in perception, too wrapped up in her own selfish world to be struck by the incongruity of such a statement even when her sister swung slightly on her heel straight into the path of a ray of Venetian sunshine spilling through the window of the *palazzo* perched upon the banks of the Grand Canal. It drew vibrant sparks from hair Titian would have itched to imitate and added extra sparkle to emerald eyes betraying at that moment a gemlike hardness as they rested upon her sister's face. As she stepped forward not even anger could dispel grace of movement from a body which at first sight seemed boyishly slim until her loose silken robe caught and

5

clung to a voluptuous curve of breast, a rounded hip and slender tapering thigh.

'Dear Sara,' she mocked, deliberately affecting the very English drawl her sister abominated, 'you have achieved your ultimate ambition, have you not? Papà has gone to a great deal of trouble to arrange a marriage between yourself and a personable Italian male. After months of behind-the-scenes negotiations between our respective families, innumerable meetings between yourself and your intended—each, I might stress, with myself as an unwilling chaperone—we have reached the stage of final negotiation when, after a meeting of both families, the contract will be signed and your intended spouse gratified by his success in manoeuvring himself within grasping distance of the Domini millions. Why then is your tongue not dripping with honey and your sharp little claws cushioned with velvet?'

Sara jumped to her feet, a black-haired, dark-eyed bundle of fury. 'You make it all sound so sordid! It isn't that way at all, you know very well that Vincente and I were attracted from the first moment of meeting.'

Jo nodded agreeably. 'An added bonus for him, considering he would have been willing to marry you had you been bow-legged, buck-toothed and peering at him through bi-focal lenses.'

Sara's volcanic temper almost reached the point of eruption. Staring down at her from her superior height, Jo registered for the umpteenth time the similarities shared by her younger sister and their

6

Italian father. Both were characteristically dark, volatile and passionately devoted to their beliefs; both were easily swayed by emotion yet conversely were possessed of a hard materialistic streak and the sort of determination that had been the prime factor behind Enrico Domini becoming one of the richest industrialists in England, a country not noted for its generosity towards down-at-heel immigrants.

'How dare you imply that Vincente is attracted only by Papà's wealth!' Sara spat. 'I know he loves me as I love him, passionately, devotedly. We live only for the day when we can be married, and it's you, heartless, selfish sister, who keeps us apart!'

'Rubbish.' Jo tossed the word across a negligent shoulder as she sauntered back towards the window.

'It is *not* rubbish!' Sara's small foot thumped down upon the carpet. 'You know very well that in Papà's family tradition decrees that the elder sister be married first—Papà insists upon it. Gratified though he is by my engagement to Vincente, he won't hear of us setting a date for the wedding until your own engagement has been announced. Oh, he *sympathises*,' she uttered a sharp, derisory laugh, at the same time flinging out her arms in a gesture of hopelessness that was entirely Latin, 'he bids us have patience. "*Wait just a little while longer, children,*" she mimicked, words rushing like a river in spate across her tongue. "*Venice, the city of Casanova, abounds with attractive men, sooner or later Jo is certain to——*" ' She jolted to a halt, just a little too late in applying a brake to her tongue. Appalled by her slip, she waited in tense silence, bracing mentally for the onslaught of a caustic tongue.

'So!' Jo's hiss was more frightening than a shout. 'Now it becomes clear why he was so insistent upon my joining you here! I, too, am to be held up for sale in the market places of Venice, dangled as a rich prize beneath the nose of every penniless nobleman in this city of stinking canals who lacks sufficient cash to keep up his standard of idle living or to maintain the rotting foundations of his crumbling pink *palazzo*!'

'No, Jo,' Sara protested, 'all Papà wishes is for you to be happy, as happy as Vincente and I, as happy as he and Mammà were . . .'

'Mammà . . .' Jo sighed, her taut features softening as memories chased brilliance from her eyes. 'I wish she were still alive—she would have championed my aversions to outmoded Italian customs.'

Relieved that the storm had been averted, Sara whispered, 'You must miss her greatly, you were so much alike. Because of my own rapport with Papà I can understand and sympathise; when Mammà died my loss was great, but yours was far greater.' She cocked her head to one side and with birdlike timidity summed up, 'You're very English, Jo, no one would believe you have a single drop of Italian blood in your veins. Everything about you is as English as was Mammà—you've inherited her red hair, her fair skin, her precise manner of speaking, her economy and grace of movement, but most of all, I think, her very logical mind. Do you remember how she used to refuse to read us fairy stories when we were children and insisted instead upon reading out

8

suitable articles from the local newspaper? She wanted us, she said, even at a very early age, to be up to date with the affairs of the country, to know about every aspect of English life. I suspect she was afraid we might become swamped by the close-knit Italian community we'd gathered up around us. Her reading used to send me to sleep, but you, Jo, used to drink in every word; I remember how you would both discuss the articles the following day. Mammà would have been pleased, too, about your choice of career; whereas Papà and I were puzzled by your choice, she would have been delighted to welcome a scientist into the family.'

Jo eyed her sister's placating face and decided to be kind. 'Liar,' she grinned, but with such lack of heat Sara was able to relax, 'you and Papà were not merely puzzled, you were appalled. Tell the truth,' she challenged, 'didn't you both decide that I'd chosen to follow an unsuitable, most unfeminine profession?'

'Well . . .' Sara's glance slid away, 'it's perhaps not so unsuitable for an Englishwoman as it would be for an Italian.'

'Exactly!' Jo stressed, the warning flicker returning to her eyes. 'I would like both of you and Papà to remember that first and foremost I'm English. You may prefer to think of yourself as an Italian and you're quite entitled to do so, providing you don't try to exert pressure upon me to do the same. So oblige me, please, by passing on that message to Papà, tell him in straight, simple terms so that he's convinced once and for all that under no circumstances could I look with favour upon an Italian husband, nor indeed upon any husband at all. At the moment marriage for me is out, there's no room for a man in the future I've planned.'

'But, Jo ...' Sara's cry was almost a wail, 'that means that Vincente and I can never marry!'

'It means nothing of the sort,' was Jo's crisp reply. 'If Signor Marvese is anything of a man he'll prove it by marrying you with or without the dowry Papà has promised him. Actually, I'm doing you a favour by putting the man to a test, his reaction will help you to honestly assess his worth.'

When Sara lapsed into sulky silence Jo returned to the window to continue her contemplation of the scene outside. The Grand Canal was lined with palaces, the one in which they were at present residing being the most pretentious. They all seemed very big, and more than once she had wondered why the Venetians were so reckless with space when their city was so small. They're show-offs, she decided, show-offs to the world to impress it with their achievements, show-offs to each other, parading in front of friends and enemies the trappings of success. How humiliated they, as a race, must have felt during their slow decline.

Her elegant nose wrinkled with distaste. The Grand Canal seemed to her a cesspit into which fifty-odd smaller canals deposited their rubbish with the rise and fall of the tide. Lines of dark damp brick ran the length of the frontages, evidence that ground floors were flooded during high spring tides. At present the tide was low, exposing slimy bottom steps and the decaying foundations of crumbling palaces.

They had arrived in Venice only a few hours earlier and she had not yet had time to examine the palace in which they were to stay for the duration of their visit. But upon their arrival, while being helped from the private motor boat that had been sent to fetch them, she had heard her father mutter his approval as he stepped on to the *campo* fronting the palace, a paved open area, the presence of which, according to him, denoted that the owner was, or his forebears had been, extremely rich or prominent noblemen, perhaps both.

She turned away from the scene that left her emotionally cold, boredom prompting her to ask, 'Who is our host, by the way—I believe he was out when we arrived?'

Sara perked up, obviously this was a subject she was eager to discuss. 'Il Conte Leandro Tempera, Vincente's cousin,' she beamed, looking for signs that Jo was impressed. 'As you know, Vincente's mother was widowed very young. The Conte's father, her elder brother, took both her and Vincente under his wing and when he died his son, Leandro, the present Conte, inherited his responsibilities. Technically he is now the head of the family and as Vincente's home is too small to accommodate us the Conte insisted that we must stay with him.'

'How very feudal!' Jo found it impossible to suppress her irritation. 'I would have preferred to stay with Nonna Domini, it seems to me ridiculous that we should impose ourselves upon a stranger when we have a grandmother living nearby.' When Sara did not reply Jo urged, 'Well, don't you agree?' Narrowly she watched her sister nervously pleating the material of her skirt in order to avoid meeting her eyes. Finally, however, when Jo's stare could no longer be suffered, Sara mumbled:

'We ... Papà and I, decided that Nònna's house wouldn't suit our purpose. We shall be expected to entertain, to return the hospitality extended by Vincente's family, and while in our present circumstances it won't seem odd to utilise the services of an hotel, if we were to stay with Nònna Domini we would naturally be expected to entertain in the family home.'

'Naturally,' Jo affirmed, her steady gaze fixed hard upon Sara's embarrassed face. 'A much more suitable solution, I would have thought.'

'Nònna is too old to be bothered,' Sara gulped.

'Nonsense, she loves having guests and you know it.'

'Her house is too small,' Sara continued desperately, 'and also it's quite some distance away ...'

Jo's honest soul revolted against such blatant prevarication. 'You damned little snob! What you really mean is that Nònna Domini's home isn't grand enough, the food which she would cook and offer to her guests with such pride would be too unpretentious for the palates of your high and mighty friends! That *you* should think along such lines is bad enough, but I'm ashamed of Papà—he has always insisted that he's proud of his humble beginnings, yet this conversation would seem to indicate that he's now so pride-ridden he would prefer to forget the mother who toiled ceaselessly to rear six sons on the wages of a Murano glassblower!'

Sara jumped to her feet, the better to defy Jo's anger. 'I love Grandmother just as much as you do, and Papà loves her even more, but he's realistic enough to acknowledge that she wouldn't fit into the society within which we now move. Call us snobbish if you like, but it's you who are a snob—an inverted snob. You've never known poverty, so why claim affinity with those who have? Nònna Domini is comfortably off, Papà has seen to it that she wants for nothing. Yet she refuses to move, even though Papà has offered many times to buy her a more comfortable house in a better neighbourhood. She's stubborn, that one! But if she insists upon clinging to her old way of life she can't object if we, in turn, want to cling to ours. Don't worry that her feelings will be hurt, Papà has gone to her house today to explain the situation and, knowing him as we do, we need have no qualms that he'll do it as tactfully as possible.'

Jo swung on her heel, heading for the door separating their adjoining rooms. The expression on her sister's face was disturbing; she was used to her fiery temper and familiarity had rendered her partially immune, but the horrified disgust Jo was displaying was something new and was causing her great unease. Could the course of action she and Papà had decided upon possibly strike others as unacceptably as it was striking Jo?

Jo's accusing voice reached her just as she was about to step out of the room. 'The true snob is never satisfied, Sara, there's always another mountain to climb and the higher you go the more people you'll be required to look down upon! Take care you're not left stranded upon your lofty peak, isolated from the warmth of humanity. If you should fall who will be there to catch you?'

'Not you, Jo!' Sara flung a last tempestuous barb, 'you'll be bent double from the weight of the chip you carry on your shoulder!'

Left alone with her sizzling thoughts, Jo paced her bedroom, sparing not a glance for the decor which, had she been in a different frame of mind, she would have found delightful. Curtains of priceless lace, delicate cream-coloured webs hanging from ceiling to floor with, here and there, minute, carefully executed darns betraying great age and loving care; matching cover and drapes on a huge four-poster bed; furniture gilded and ornate with legs carved into a semblance of such fragility they looked incapable of bearing weight. Keeping her eyes riveted upon the carpet, she paced, crushing masses of blue bell-shaped flowers beneath her feet, grounding fullblown roses beneath her furious heel.

The insult to her grandmother had cut deep. Jo, above all, was loyal to her family and her friends. She felt sickened and ashamed of the attitude adopted by Sara and her father, so much so that she felt tempted to pack her bags and leave. But such action would be taken as an affront by Vincente's family, so that course of action was out; angry though she was with her sister she could not deliberately set out to destroy her happiness. Later that evening—she checked her watch—in less than an hour, in fact, the two families were due to dine together at the *palazzo*. Once that hurdle had been vaulted perhaps she would be able to fade into the background, visit Nònna for a few days, then quietly depart for England.

The decision made, she decided in her usual impetuous fashion that her father must be told. Immediately she sped from her room in search of him, running along carpeted corridors, down a wide sweep of stairs, then jerked to a halt in the centre of a huge hall wondering which of the many doors was hiding him from view. He was bound to be back by now, dinner was less than an hour away, so, being punctilious in his habits, she was sure he would have left himself plenty of time to dress for the occasion. He was not in his room, she had checked there first, which meant that he had to be somewhere downstairs.

Her ear caught the murmur of voices. She spun round then like a bloodhound on the scent headed towards the sound, judging that it was coming from behind a heavy wooden door that had been left just a crack ajar. As she hesitated, wondering whether to walk in or to knock, she recognised Vincente's slightly accented voice.

'The elder sister is *una seccatura*—a nuisance—as Sara describes her. Although aware that her father will not allow our wedding to take place until her own engagement has been announced, she flatly refuses to give up her career in favour of marriage.'

'So?' a masculine voice filled with an amusement that set Jo's teeth on edge enquired. 'And what is this career upon which the *signorina* sets such store?'

'She wishes to become a scientist. Her goal is still some three years away because she is as yet still studying at university. Can you imagine,' Vincente's voice rose at the injustice, 'Sara and me having to wait three whole years simply to accommodate this obstinate sister?'

'Unnatural,' the other voice sympathised. 'It occurs to me, however, that there might be a simpler reason why this sister remains unmarried. Could it be possible that she has never yet been approached by any man with matrimony in mind? Personally, I would feel very reluctant to ask a scientist to share my bed; it would require a rare breed of man to make love to a brain machine. Would you not yourself search out a fragrant, willing bundle of femininity if ever the need were upon you?'

'Someone like Francesca, you mean?' Vincente suggested slyly, laughter spilling into his voice.

'Certainly not!' The stern reply implied that Vincente had overstepped the mark. 'Francesca's name has no place in such a discussion!'

Without waiting to hear Vincente's stammered apology Jo fled with ears burning, flags of dangerous colour high upon her cheeks. Once back in her room she leant against the door, fighting wild anger jabbing along every nerve, her body so tense it ached.

'*Animal!*' she hissed denunciation of the unknown male. 'Arrogant, supercilious *beast*!' She clenched her fists, wishing it were possible to defend herself physically against his sneers, furious at having been made the butt of jibes he would not tolerate in connection with a woman of his own race. 'Francesca, whoever she might be, is welcome to him!'

CHAPTER TWO

Half an hour later Jo, looking outwardly serene, was ready to join the guests assembling downstairs. Sara and her father had both rapped upon her door in passing, urging her to hurry, but as she had a special reason for making a late entrance she had bidden them both to carry on without her. She waited until she was certain that all the guests had arrived before moving towards the door, sustained by an icy calm, having no need to check her appearance in any of the many mirrors she passed on her way downstairs.

Upon reaching the main salon she stood poised in the doorway, waiting to be noticed.

Conversation was rippling from many tongues, bright, curious eyes were resting upon Sara and Vincente who were standing just inside the doorway with their backs turned towards her, flanked either side by Enrico, beaming a proud father's smile, and a taller, slimmer figure with dinner jacket set impeccably upon broad shoulders, dark sleeves baring an exact amount of cuff around brown, sinewy wrists and the back of a head held with such assurance she knew instinctively that she was looking at the owner of the unknown voice.

There was a gasp of surprise, then a second and yet a third before conversation dribbled into silence.

Simultaneously four backs turned, seeking the cause of the diversion, and four pairs of eyes lit upon Jo leaning casually against the door jamb wearing ancient jeans rolled up above the knees to show an expanse of multi-coloured woollen sock rising from feet encased in grubby sandals; a vivid orange tee-shirt with I AM A BITCH scrawled in black letters across its front, and two hideous green ribbons tied around hair parted from back to front and gathered into two untidy bunches that hung down across each shoulder. Nonchalantly she stared into their outraged faces, then poked the tip of her tongue between lips slashed with purple lipstick, puffed out her cheeks and blew hard until a pink balloon of bubble-gum almost obscured her face.

'*Jo, how could you!*' Sara's rebuke, blasted on an icy breath, connected with the fragile bubble and it burst, splattering gum all around Jo's mouth. Easily, she scraped it off, wiped her hand across the seat of her jeans, then offered it to the intently watching stranger.

'You must be the Conte. How do you do, I'm Josephine, Sara's sister.'

She was disappointed when amusement tugged up the corners of his mouth before an urbane mask was donned. Politely he bowed across her sticky hand before replying in faultless English. 'How do you do, *signorina*. I am enchanted to meet you.'

'Oh ...' When disconcertion clamped her throat she swallowed hard, floundering desperately for words with which to pierce his hateful composure, but was left stranded by a brain that went blank and a tongue that refused to be prised from the roof of her mouth.

The first joust had undoubtedly gone .to the Conte!

Her father's anger was her salvatiŏn. With a muttered, *'Scusi, signore,'* he grasped Jo tightly by the elbow and marched her out of sight of the scandalised looks being cast by the members of Vincente's family. Her feet barely touched the ground as she was propelled towards a small ante-room where once inside he kicked shut the door before exploding:

'I want an explanation for your disgraceful behaviour—and I warn you, Jo, it had better be convincing!' He was very angry! Jo suffered a qualm. With true Venetian intensity Enrico Domini loved his children and had, especially since their mother's death, indulged them disgracefully. Never before had she been the recipient of the ruthless determination that had made him succeed in business where lesser men might have failed. They had always been honest with each other, however, so, though trembling in her shoes, Jo bravely admitted:

'What I did was a gesture of protest against snobbery! When Sara told me about your plan to keep Nònna apart from Vincente's family I felt sick with disgust and terribly ashamed of both of you.'

Her father folded his arms across his chest, his expression grim. 'So in your usual hot-headed manner you decided to retaliate, without even waiting to discuss the situation. You made a spectacle of yourself by appearing dressed as a ragamuffin before people who set great store upon grace and beauty.

In the whole of Venice you will not find a woman or a girl in such a state of utter *déshabille*. That outfit,' his glance seared, 'might not elevate an eyebrow in the university cities of England, but here women would not be seen dead in trousers—the only slovenly people in the whole of Venice are tourists—yet you disgrace me and your sister by coming down to dinner in an outfit that would make a housemaid shudder! Though you are twenty-three years of age, Jo, and Sara merely eighteen, I sometimes think she is twice as mature as you are.'

Jo blanched, unspeakably hurt, not so much by the words which she knew were deserved but by the tone of voice in which they had been delivered. Her father's florid but still handsome face blurred. Quickly she blinked away tears before returning to the attack.

'You had no right to snub Nònna Domini,' she choked, 'she's worth a hundred of those pampered remnants of an extinct nobility!'

'Do you think me unaware of that fact?' His question rang cold with distaste. 'If you had given me the chance I would have explained that your grandmother has made herself quite ill with the worry of having to entertain large numbers of strangers with whom she has nothing in common. She wrote to me while we were still in England, ex-explaining her fears and begging to be excused the duty of playing hostess to Vincente's many relatives. She is old and she is tired; for those very reasons I felt qualms about asking her to take on such an

21

onerous task in the first place, but because it is customary and because I would not for the world have my mother feel slighted I did ask her, Jo.'

She stared, appalled, then ran to crumple against his chest almost choking with remorse. 'I'm so sorry I misjudged you, Papà, I ought to have known better.'

Kind arms cradled her until her tears were spent, then prising her shamed face from his shoulder he looked down and sadly shook his head. 'What is to be done with you, Jo? Some day I fear your hasty tongue will bring you great grief. You must learn to control your temper, child, to think long and hard before you speak, especially,' his voice took on a warning note, 'when you apologise to the Conte.'

'Apologise to the Conte!' She wrenched out of his arms. 'I shall do no such thing!'

'But you will,' he insisted thinly, 'that is, if you wish to continue studying towards the career you profess to value so much. The British government is good to its students, it provides grants for books, for living accommodation, and education is free, but as its coffers are not entirely bottomless parents have to help out. You will find it very difficult, if not impossible, to carry on without an allowance. The choice is yours, Jo—either apologise to the Conte for your appalling bad manners or face a future full of stringent economies.'

She glared, barely able to believe that this hard-eyed, stern-faced man was the same parent who in the past had indulged her every whim. What he had said was true, she could not manage without the allowance he made her. She could wave the banner of independence by telling him to keep his money, but honesty forced her to acknowledge the impossibility of surviving without his financial help within a society where inflation was rampant.

Her reply was rebellious, but her tone was such that he knew the argument had been won. 'You wish to teach me a lesson in humility, Papà, is that it?'

'Such a lesson would do you no harm,' he admitted, edging nearer a mood of affability, 'but mainly I wish the Conte to receive what is his due.' He seemed prepared to carry on lecturing at length, but to Jo's relief the sound of the dinner gong penetrated the room. 'I must go, the other guests must not be kept waiting. I'll make apologies for your absence, of course, and ask the Conte to spare five minutes of his time once the meal is over. Meanwhile, I suggest you go to your room, clean the mess from your face, and don a dress suitable for your meeting with the Conte.' His tone became droll. 'An up-to-date version of sackcloth and ashes might be appropriate ...'

'Very funny!' Jo fumed when her father had left the room, glaring wildly around at surroundings that seemed suddenly to have adopted an ambience of a penitent's cell. 'Apologise to that ... that! Oh, *hell*!' She spun on her heel like a furious top, then charged upstairs to her room.

After writhing for an hour with the agonies of defeat she reluctantly admitted herself beaten, scrubbed her face, applied a light film of make-up, arranged her hair into a neat red cap, then, in a wry gesture of deference to her father's wishes, chose a dove-grey dress, its severity softened only by a white collar and childishly prim cuffs. She then sat by the window and waited, her mind a blank, until a maidservant knocked upon the door to inform her that the Conte was waiting for her in his study.

A true Venetian is instantly recognisable by his features, Jo decided as she stepped into the book-lined room and began walking towards a figure seated behind a huge, heavily carved desk. He stood up immediately she entered and motioned her to a chair, waiting until she was comfortable before resuming his own seat.

'Your father tells me you wish to speak to me, *signorina*?' She noted the slightly calculating look in his dark eyes and the enigmatical twist lifting the corners of his mouth. His blade-straight nose was that of a Renaissance prince, she criticised, disliking his air of condescension, mistrusting the guile hidden behind dark, almost oriental features, probably inherited from some long-distant ancestor. She stirred, made uncomfortable by his keen assessment. 'You look very different, it is hard to believe that you are the same girl I met earlier this evening— *bellissima*, in fact.' This was stated without flourish or flattery, casually flung, as if barely interested. Perversely she felt annoyed.

'My father considers I owe you an apology.'

He digested the bald statement, then, smiling slightly, suggested, 'Your father may, but obviously you do not?'

She blushed, recognising rebuke, then jumped to

24

her feet. 'I'm sorry if I sounded curt, *signore*. Please accept my apologies for any embarrassment I may have caused either you or your guests.' She half swung away, but his quiet request detained her.

'Please don't go, *signorina*. Like you, I consider an apology unnecessary—however, there is another matter I would like to discuss.' He waved her back to the chair she had vacated. 'If you would spare me a few more minutes of your time?'

Surprised, she resumed her seat, but perched on the edge, wary as a sparrow suspecting the motives of a prowling cat.

'Will you smoke?' He proffered a silver cigarette box, withdrawing it when she shook her head. 'Not many of my countrywomen indulge in the habit, but I know the emancipated English female is fond of her cigarettes. I believe you are one of those liberated women, a strict upholder of the view that modern woman is entitled to be free to follow her own destiny even if that freedom is detrimental to the happiness of her less liberated sister?'

The gist of his remarks became immediately clear. 'Why flirt with words, *signore*? If you think I am being selfish because I choose to ignore my father's old-fashioned decree that I must marry before my sister why don't you come right out and say so? But before you do, let me warn you first that you will be wasting your time. I feel no compunction whatsoever about following my chosen career because, if I were in Sara's shoes, I would go ahead and marry if I were as much in love as she professes to be, with or without my father's permission. The only stumbling block, so far as I am aware, is Vincente's reluctance to go against my father's wishes. That, I interpret not so much as an unwillingness on his part to upset my father's feelings, as a fear that he might become estranged from the Domini fortune.'

If she had thought to rouse him to anger she was disappointed. He levelled a long cool look, slowly digesting every facet of her appearance, his eyes sliding downward from her vital red head, tempestuous green eyes, anger-flushed cheeks, then remained lingering thoughtfully upon a passionate mouth set stern to stem further furious words.

'You are very insulting,' he told her without heat, his dark eyes morose. 'Towards your sister, that is. Sara is so beautiful, so charming, how can you possibly doubt Vincente's love for her?'

'I would doubt any Venetian's capacity to love. You are not a warm people, *signore*. You are a passionless race, excited only by possessions and by the envy of those with less worldly goods— mercenary beyond belief. Shylocks who break hearts without compunction when in search of their pound of flesh. Even traditional serenades, warbled with such touching pathos by your romantic gondoliers, are basically Neapolitan. There are no genuine Venetian love songs because Venetians have never learnt how to love.'

A smile flitted across lips that had grown gradually sterner while he listened to her tirade. His voice held no anger when almost lazily he protested, 'Come now, *signorina*, are you not forgetting that

26

Casanova, the greatest lover of all times, was a Venetian?'

'Indeed not,' she retorted. 'Casanova was certainly a true Venetian—cold-hearted, licentious and fickle!'

He stood up to tower over her. 'It would seem that you have formed a very unfavourable impression of my race during the short time you have been in Venice. Which is how long . . .?'

She jumped up, the better to combat his encroaching shadow. She felt smothered by his geniality, his refusal to be riled, and irritated by the suspicion that secretly he was laughing at her. 'Mere hours,' she admitted sharply, 'but I have lived a lifetime with your traditions and taboos, have served a long and painful apprenticeship until I now feel qualified to claim myself an expert at seeing through your pretences.'

'Some people, Signorina Domini, see only what they wish to see, believe only what they wish to believe. Women are especially prone to this, especially women who are at war with themselves, women who fight to suppress their femininity, who are ashamed of the vulnerabilities of their sex and who, because they are neither physically nor mentally equipped to take up the burdens borne by men, finally turn against the sex they initially tried to ape. *Poverina!* Your father has confessed to me how much he regrets the absence of a son—subconsciously, even during childhood, you must have been trying to fill this void in his life. But by adopting an aggressive attitude you have not supplied him with a son but merely denied him a daughter—one about whose virtues he could rave, one whose sweet disposition would make him the envy of his cronies. As it has turned out, you are simply an embarrassment to him, a bad-tempered wench whose chances of matrimony are depleted each time she exercises her shrewish tongue!'

She stepped back, outraged. This, too, was characteristic of the devious Venetian—the deceptively mild approach used as a matador would use his cloak to conceal the weapon poised to deliver an unexpectedly cruel thrust.

'How dare you!' she gasped, groping for further words of scorn to heap upon his unrepentant head. Her chin lifted so that he was directly in line with twin daggers of danger trained upon his face. 'I could marry any man I choose!' she challenged, throwing down the gauntlet. 'Any Venetian, that is! There is not a man in this city of merchants that my father could not buy for me. No doubt,' she continued in her impetuous fashion, unaware of betraying bewilderment and hurt, 'my father is at this very moment offering me up for sale. Indeed, Sara has already let it slip that he brought me to Venice with the specific intention of finding me a husband! He has lectured me on my wilfulness, Sara hardly lets a moment pass without heaping recriminations upon my head and now you, too, have had your say! I ask you, *signore*, would you give up your freedom, revise your way of thinking, enter into marriage with a complete stranger, simply to indulge another person's whim?'

She was aggravated by the slow, deliberate attention he gave to the question and was made extremely uncomfortable by the dark stare that seemed to penetrate mental and physical barriers in search of truth.

'I might,' he answered slowly, as if still deliberating, 'depending on how much regard I felt for the person concerned.'

She took his reply as a rebuke, a rebuke which, coupled with all the earlier aggravations of the day, prodded from her a reckless challenge.

'Very well, *signore*, I'll give you the chance to prove your words! You say you're concerned about Sara's and Vincente's happiness; you've condemned as selfish my refusal to be sacrificed upon the altar of matrimony and you've professed that you would not stand in their way if you were in my shoes. I think you're a sanctimonious, lying prig, and for that very reason I feel no fear of putting you to the test ... You have my solemn promise that I will marry, *signore*, just as swiftly as the wedding can be arranged.'

For once she had managed to surprise him. His eyebrows shot up, his expression a mixture of puzzlement and satisfaction. She held his look, savouring her triumph before slowly spelling out her condition of surrender.

'Providing, *signore*,' she stressed with mockery, *'that you agree to be my bridegroom!'*

CHAPTER THREE

HER wedding dress, they told her, had been hand-stitched over a century ago by nuns of a famous order. The wreath which was to hold in place the matching ivory veil was of pure gold, beaten wafer-thin, then fashioned into finely-veined ivy leaves.

Crossly Jo tried it on, then tossed a derisory glance at her reflection in a mirror. 'It makes me look like ruddy Nero!' she muttered, jerking her head so that the wreath slipped, its sharp pointed leaves digging into her forehead. 'How could you allow yourself to fall into such a trap, idiot!' she asked fiercely of her mutinous reflection. 'Your challenge must have loomed like manna from heaven before the impoverished Conte. What in heaven's name impelled you to call his bluff?'

At the sound of footsteps progressing towards her room she snatched off the wreath and flung it on to the bed. She was standing staring out of the window when Sara bounced in.

'I've just been talking to Leo; he would like to see you as soon as you can spare the time. Naturally, I told him you would come immediately I passed on his message.'

'Did you now!' Jo drawled, not bothering to turn her head. 'Why, I wonder, did you think I would drop everything and run immediately to answer the Conte's bidding?'

'Because,' Sara gave an exasperated shrug, 'he is the Conte, I suppose. Though his attitude never demands it, he does command a certain degree of deference from most people.'

'Not from me!' Jo's heel ground into the carpet as she swung round to challenge her sister. 'The man's nature is as shallow as his purse, and his utterances as meaningless as his title. I've told both you and Father how he tricked me into agreeing to be his wife, and if he insists upon keeping me to my word I'll make life so unbearable for him that before many months have passed he'll be clamouring at the doors of the Vatican begging a special dispensation in order to obtain his freedom!'

Blithely Sara tripped over to the bed and picked up the wreath of golden leaves that was to be Jo's crown of thorns. 'Serves you right!' she smiled her complacency. 'You asked for everything you've got and I for one feel no sympathy for you. Papà warned you many times that your tongue would run you into trouble your feet could not walk you out of, and it's happened just as he predicted.'

'I was only trying to prove what a hypocrite the man is!' Jo protested vehemently. 'How was I to guess he would drag me in front of all his relatives, giving me no time whatsoever to protest, then announce with great ceremony that I'd promised to be his wife! The gall of the creature!' Her mind shuddered from the memory of the nightmare that had been enacted the previous evening. 'He knew I had no real intention of marrying him, yet he gave me no chance to back out of my idiot promise.'

'Nor will he ever.' Sara's satisfied-cat smile was very much in evidence. 'Actually,' she ran a speculative look over her sister's tense body, 'I don't think he has any more wish to marry than you have, but he has Vincente's well-being in mind. Leo has always taken his responsibilities seriously; he probably feels that as he's head of the Tempera family it is his duty to resolve the problems of all its members even if as a consequence he has to sacrifice his freedom. Such a man will make an ideal husband, Jo—a better husband than you deserve, in fact.'

'But I don't *want* a husband!' Jo lashed back, fuming with impotent anger. 'Not even one who's a paragon of virtue, or as rich as Onassis, or as handsome as Omar Sharif! Still less do I want to become the wife of a mercenary Count who's no doubt weighed up very carefully and concluded that his crumbling *palazzo* will benefit from the support of Papà's cheque book!'

'Leo is far too proud——' Sara began hotly, then was left addressing an empty room as Jo raced past, her back held rigid with resentment.

Jo went in search of the Conte and found him in his study. She rushed inside and without preamble began her protest. 'Now listen to me, this comedy of errors must be terminated immediately!'

'Comedy of errors?' He rose to his feet, twirling a pen between languid fingers. 'Is that a proper way to describe our imminent marriage, *bella*?'

'Don't call me Bella, my name is Jo!'

Her pretended obtuseness did not deceive him. He laughed aloud. 'Bella—beautiful. Yes, it is much more appropriate than the masculine-sounding Jo.' When he stepped forward she hastily backed away, but was not quick enough to elude the determined hand that fastened upon her shoulder. Held firm, she had to suffer his touch as he entwined a frond of hair wisping her forehead around his lean finger. 'May I?' he enquired. Before she realised his intention he had swooped upon a pair of scissors lying on his desk and snipped off the curl, retaining it in the palm of his hand. He released her shoulder to brood down at the red-gold circle lying like a brand of fire against his palm, then he eased from an inner pocket a flat leather case which he handed to her, instructing, 'Open it, please.'

It sprang apart at her touch, revealing twin lockets nestling side by side upon a bed of white velvet. They looked so incredibly unique she could not suppress a gasp of admiration. Each golden locket was fashioned into the image of a lion—the symbol of the Tempera family whose eldest son was always christened Leonardo, after the king of the jungle. Bushy-maned, with wickedly curving tails, their golden eyes stared jewel-bright, a hard, unblinking stare uncannily like that of the man waiting silently for her reaction. In the centre of each leonine body was a carved glass profile set within four golden claws, one was of a man with classic Roman features, the other a gentler, less severe profile of a girl bearing upon her head a minute replica

33

of the golden wreath each Tempera bride wore on her wedding day.

In silence, Leo lifted from its bed of velvet the locket bearing the girl's profile, pressed a hidden spring, and when it sprang open to reveal a cavity he placed inside Jo's lock of hair. He then snapped it shut and slipped it into his pocket.

'The other one you will retain in your possession,' he indicated with a nod the remaining locket. 'Anticipating your request for a lock of my hair, I have already obliged. These are traditional betrothal gifts,' he carried on urbanely, impervious, it seemed, to her astonished stare. 'For many centuries Tempera lovers have exchanged these lockets containing either a portrait or some personal memento. I will provide you with a wedding ring, of course, but in my family the exchanging of these lockets has always been considered more binding than the actual marriage ceremony. You might almost say,' he tossed her a smile full of whimsy, 'that from this moment on I shall regard you as my bride. Our marriage will not be consummated until after the church ceremony, of course,' he thoughtfully reassured her, 'but so far as I am concerned you are now the Contessa Josephine Tempera. I hope,' he reached out a hand to raise her nerveless fingers to his lips, 'that we will share a long and happy association, *bella moglie*.'

The endearment broke her trance. She sprang away, putting a yard of carpet between them. 'I am not your beautiful spouse, *signore*, not yet! And I promise you that if you insist upon keeping me to my word you'll regret it every day, every hour, every moment of the time we're together. I'm not so gullible as my young sister who fondly believes that her fiancé is captivated by her charms. I suffer under no such illusion! I'm very well aware that the motive behind your own and Vincente's eagerness to marry us is the healthy state of our father's wallet. However,' she dared another desperate bluff, 'if you are still prepared to suffer the consequences then by all means let us marry. But mark this, *signore*, you will not be treated by me as a husband, there will be no tender exchanges between us and certainly no wild nights of passion. I will accept you only as a *cicisbeo* —knowing how conversant you are with ancient Venetian customs I need not outline what your duties will be.' When his lips thinned she experienced a thrill of triumph. Good! At last she had managed to penetrate his insufferable *politesse*, the restrained decorum that was so much a part of the Venetian character. Fired with success, she adopted a more confident, almost cocky manner.

'I was quite surprised, when researching your history, to learn that in eighteenth-century Venice most women were liberated, at least sexually, and were absolutely free to do exactly as they pleased. According to the books I read most of them made the most of it. Each woman, besides having a tolerant husband, had her *cicisbeo*, her recognised companion. After the first year of marriage she was free to choose such a companion with the full consent of her husband, the only provision being that he should be her social equal. I shan't impose upon you duties that are too onerous, *signore*. I shall ex-

35

pect you to attend me constantly, carry any parcels I might gather up while shopping, help me into my gondola, accompany me to the opera and take me to see whatever I might express a wish to see, but I will forgo the pleasure of having you kiss my hand each time we meet.' Quite carried away by a sensation of power, she waited with feet astride, her look challenging him to an argumentative duel. If the Conte was determined to enjoy the feel of her father's purse he must also suffer the lash of her whip.

For a long breathless moment while her gaze was held by a cold golden glitter unpleasantly reminiscent of the jewelled lion's stare, she thought her challenge was about to be met. Silence lengthened. The room seemed suddenly to chill. She trembled a little, reminded of the Venetian's devotion, amounting almost to obsession, with the beasts of the jungle. The city was crammed with their stone images, winged lions, aloof lions, fierce lions, lions supporting windows, outstretched on doorsteps, even climbing chimneys and stuck on flowerpots and garden gates. They were carved out of wood, stone, immortalised in oils, and stamped upon leather. Uneasily she recalled a remark she had heard passed about the Venetian character. '*It is understandable that the Venetian should so greatly admire the powerful beast, for bestial too are the men of Venice when the madness of revenge grips them!*'

She jerked away, turning her back upon the silent man who seemed filled with an anger that could rend. She had to escape the ambience of menace filling the room, for the first time her young, coura-

36

geous spirit was fearful, a fear that quickened her footsteps, that elevated her heart from her breast so that it was trapped, a soaring, panic-stricken prisoner in her throat.

'One moment, please! We have not yet finished our discussion.' The command was crisp, decisive, yet held no threat. She halted, then spun slowly on her heel wondering, as her quick eyes noted the half-smile curving his lips and his negligent ease of movement, how she could ever have suspected him of savagery. She experienced an inexplicable pang of disappointment. The lion was but a lamb ...

This assumption was responsible for her tone of sharp contempt when she addressed him. 'If you're about to say that you've changed your mind about marrying me, *signore*, I shall be only too pleased to listen.'

'On the contrary,' he replied with such mildness of manner she gritted her teeth, 'I consider that we are ideally suited. Besides,' he rebuked gently, 'have I not just said that so far as I am concerned you already belong to me? No, I merely wish to ascertain that you fully understand the outrageousness of the condition you have just outlined. Are you aware, for instance, that more often than not the eighteenth-century *cicisbeo* was a fop, an unfortunate person who, because he lacked his share of hormones, was more at home in the company of women than of men from whom he received little sympathy and towards whom he felt no affinity? The luckless creature found women tolerant of his shortcomings providing he remained willing to fetch and carry for them, to lend an attentive ear to their troubles, was ever ready to ease a headache by dabbing a cologne-soaked handkerchief on to a pained brow. Husbands were tolerant, as you said. They could afford to be because there was never any danger of their being cuckolded by these creatures. Sex between a woman and her *cicisbeo* was so rare as to be almost non-existent. Even today, the *cicisbeo* has his counterpart in the drawing-rooms of wealthy women all over the world. In France they are named gigolos; I do not know if there is a word for them in your country.' His unusual golden eyes glinted with amusement as he challenged, 'Tell me truthfully, Jo, do you really believe that I fit into that category?'

Her lips parted to utter a confirmatory insult, but all that escaped was a hissing sigh as she met disquietening eyes, piercing, yet with a hint of pity in their depths that caused her to swallow hard. He did not move a finger, did not utter a word, yet she was very much aware of masculine assurance emanating from his lean body. Vital black hair sprang from his forehead, tutored into neatness by a brush yet hinting that, raked through by fingers, it could erupt into a wilful mass of curls. Thrusting, wide, arrogant nostrils. Eyes—cat-golden. The sensuous, rangy animal stride.

When he growled a half-laugh she had to concede, 'No, I must admit that you do not. But in any case,' she continued sharply, 'it hardly matters, your sexual prowess, or lack of it, does not interest me. All I want to know is whether, in return for the very substantial dowry my father has promised, you intend to accept the conditions I've put forward?'

'But of course,' he agreed lightly, 'it shall be my pleasure to humour you—at least for the time being.'

'For the time being will suit me fine,' she spat. 'Our alliance will last only as long as it takes to lull Papà into a sense of security and so allow my sister to achieve her objective. I have tried to dissuade her from marrying your cousin, have used every argument I know to prevent her from making what I consider would be the biggest mistake of her life, but she won't listen. She must therefore find her own solution when she eventually discovers—as she most certainly will—that I'm right and she's wrong!'

'It matters a great deal to you that you should be proved right, *poverina*, does it not?'

Condescension, coming as it did from a man whose motives she despised, was galling. 'I believe in following my own instincts,' Jo retorted. 'Once I've made up my mind about a person I'm very seldom proved to be mistaken in my judgment.'

'You are a wilful, stubborn creature.' His easy smile had slipped. 'However, I do not intend to indulge your appetite for sparring. You are a child still, Jo, and with children one has to have patience —a bitter plant that yields sweet fruit.'

'Be as patient as you like,' she retorted rudely, 'the only fruit you'll pluck will be a lemon!' She stalked out of the room with his laughter ringing in her ears, seething, yet finding time to wonder why the man she so despised, whose actions filled her with contempt, whose mercenary aims she found so distasteful, should have the power to force her to scrabble for cool disdain and be able to arouse her emotions to such white heat that whenever they came into contact she felt a savage urge to inflict pain. She was dismayed by the hatred he aroused in her. If she could keep cool she could cope. Hampered by passion, she was very, very, vulnerable ...

CHAPTER FOUR

THE next day Jo put the Conte's patience to the test. After breakfast he sought her out and found her staring gloomily out of a window overlooking the Grand Canal. Oblivious of his presence, she was murmuring to herself, 'Streets full of water, nothing but streets full of water!' likening the turgid canal to a huge artery from which smaller canals sprang like veins. It was a working day and the waterways teemed with traffic ferrying workmen about their day-to-day duties, refuse barges, parcel-post boats, ambulance boats, milk boats, even a hearse, intermingling with private motor launches, sleek speedboats and, of course, the inevitable gondola. She traced the progress of a *vaporetto*, a green and black painted motorbus lying low in the water with its full complement of passengers. Behind it chugged a cumbersome fruit barge piled high with oranges and great bunches of bananas and in its shadow a solitary man laboriously propelling a skiff full of vegetables he was no doubt hoping to sell in some city market-place.

'Good morning, Jo!' His voice startled her. 'Sara tells me you have no pressing appointment until later today, so as I am free myself I decided now would be a good time to take you on a tour of our city.' Glancing over her shoulder, he observed with a smile, 'Like most visitors, you must be appalled by the congestion and seemingly haphazard progress of our water traffic, but I assure you that you will be quite safe. Accidents, when they do occur, are usually minor. The watermen of Venice are fairly proficient—as they ought to be after fifteen centuries of practice.'

'How disappointing.' Her answering drawl contained the very essence of boredom. 'A squabble between bargemen might have helped to relieve a little of the monotony.'

'Do not despair, *vespa*,' his mouth tightened with asperity, 'I'm sure that with little effort on your part you will find plenty to complain about.'

Satisfied that he was needled, she purred, 'You may fetch my coat and bag—you can't mistake the ones I want, they're laid out on my bed.'

If she had flicked his pride he did not show it. Calmly he walked across the room to press an imperious finger upon a bell. In a matter of seconds a young maidservant tapped lightly upon the door before entering the room.

'You rang, *signore*?'

'Yes, Maria, the *signorina* would like her coat and handbag fetched from her bedroom.'

'*Si, signore*.' She bobbed a curtsey and spun round to leave, but was halted in her tracks by Jo's sharp command.

'Don't bother, Maria, the *signore* will do it. Please return to your duties.'

'*Scusi, signorina* . . . ?' The girl seemed turned to stone, her face a picture of incredulity.

'You heard what I said!' Jo's voice rang with impatience.

Timid though she was the girl hesitated, then swung pleading eyes upon the Conte, seeking guidance from the tall figure rigid with sudden hauteur. Then, within the blink of an eyelid, hauteur was gone and to the girl's amazement his calm voice instructed, 'You may go, Maria, I will fetch the *signorina*'s things myself.'

When he followed the girl out of the room Jo's teeth bit deeply into her lip. She ought to have been feeling triumphant—after all, she had successfully demonstrated her authority over the despicable Conte. But it was a Pyrrhic victory—one that left her with a sick feeling in the pit of her stomach and a shamed conviction that, to one girl at least, she represented all that was undesirable in a future *contessa*. However, she could not afford the luxury of qualms at this stage. Already the wedding was being organised—she had less than a month in which to make the Conte change his mind!

When Leo returned he made no reference to her appalling attitude but silently helped her on with her coat before suggesting gravely, 'There is a breeze blowing today, if you have a headscarf I suggest you wear it, otherwise your hair will be blown into disarray.'

Her fingers closed around a silken square in her pocket, yet perversely she chose to ignore his advice and stalked with chin outthrust outside on to the *campo*.

In common with most *palazzi*, two mooring posts,

43

striped red and white like barbers' poles, had been erected beside the landing stage with, attached to one, a black-lacquered, gold-embossed gondola bearing the twin-lion crest of the Tempera family upon its elegant swan-necked prow. The Conte bypassed this to hand Jo into a sleek, high-powered motorboat, an expensive toy which nevertheless seemed to skulk in the shadow of its aristocratic counterpart. Leo seemed to sense her disappointment when, with a quiet chuckle, he observed:

'Had my companion been Sara, I would not have hesitated to use the gondola, but knowing your preference is for the functional as opposed to the merely decorative I'm sure you approve my choice.'

'Quite correct,' she agreed coolly, 'also my preference for the useful applies not only to objects but also to men.'

He was impossible to snub, she fumed as, guiding the craft between a myriad vessels, he kept up a cheerful and informative commentary as they travelled the length of the canal, dodging between heavy barges, slicing through gaps so narrow she many times held her breath until they were safely through, sometimes exchanging good-natured badinage with other navigators while negotiating a jam, other times speeding along a clear stretch of water, foam churning in their wake, the small boat bouncing on top of the waves with a vigour she felt certain was deliberately manufactured. But if he was hoping to hear her complain he was disappointed; she would have drowned without a murmur rather than allow him to think his sneaking, underhanded effort at revenge was having the desired effect.

When, with a flourish that sent the waters of the canal into a frenzy, he drew up at a landing stage she was breathless, flushed and visibly windswept. Her knees shook as he helped her out of the boat on to solid ground, but with an irritable shrug she declined his helping hand and walked unsteadily towards a towering oriental façade that might have been transported straight out of the Arabian Nights.

Glittering gold mosaics executed by Byzantine artists above portals and windows were surrounded by sculptures representing the signs of the zodiac, the Saints and the prophets. Fanciful marble inlays, alabaster statues, gilded weathervanes and petrified palm trees, lilies, grapes, pomegranates, birds and plumes were encrusted on every available bit of space. It was overwhelming—too much of everything, so that the eye became satiated and beauty began to appear grotesque.

'Well?' he murmured in her ear. 'What are your first impressions of St Mark's?' His tone rang with characteristic pride. To the true Venetian there was no city to compare with his, no sculpture so finely executed, no paintings so vivid, no art treasures so costly or beautiful as those gathered into this city of seafarers and merchants who, in past centuries, had plundered the world.

Jo took great pleasure in voicing her opinion. 'It looks like the brainchild of some mad oriental warlord. As a whole it's certainly not beautiful, in fact, I consider it's tawdry—like the den of a robber who has stolen what he has been told is rare and costly but which, once it's in his possession, he has neither the taste nor refinement to display to best advantage.'

'Come now,' his tone was even, 'you are judging with a biased eye. Here,' he pulled her into a patch of shade, 'narrow your eyes against the light and consider again the marble veneers. See how a shower of rain has cast over them a lustrous film, as if the walls were coated with oiled silk.'

'I'm sorry,' she shrugged out of his grasp, 'to me, it still looks ugly.'

'We will return again tomorow.' He sounded on the verge of exasperation. 'St Mark's, indeed all of Venice, can be likened to a neurotic female, one day appearing lovely as a dream and the next wearing a waspish frown.' When he took her by the arm and began propelling her away from the object of his pride she sensed with glee that he was annoyed. This being so, she decided to press home her advantage.

'I see no reason,' she gasped, having to run to keep up with his stride, 'why you Venetians should expect everyone to adopt the same set of values as yourselves. For example, you state that Venice can be as beautiful as a dream, yet one person's dream can be another's nightmare. Of what does a city of Shylocks dream? Of a sun fashioned out of gold? A moon of solid silver? Showers of diamonds, pools of emeralds, mountains filled with precious minerals, earth that yields a hidden treasure trove? Not everyone,' she scoffed, 'finds pleasure in a miser's horde!'

He stopped suddenly on a narrow bridge spanning an oily eel of canal and spun her round to face him. There was a strange glint in his cat-gold eyes—a warning of a somnolent beast being prodded too far?

'There could be some truth in what you say, little *vespa*,' he snorted, 'the more I am in your company the more I think my judgment could be faulty.'

She grinned, appreciating his choice of adjective. Little wasp! A wasp could aggravate. Its sting, though seldom lethal, could cause great annoyance even to creatures many times its size.

His grip upon her chin was so unexpected she bit her tongue and for a second the pain was so intense she could have cried. 'When I first saw you I thought I saw beauty beneath the mask of paint you had daubed over your face. You were a young, immature child, I thought, locked inside the body of a woman, a body of ripe, tantalising curves that would not be disguised even by hideous garments. I felt sympathy for what I imagined was a brave attempt to attack authority, for the resentment of an independent spirit being curbed. Your attitude was defiant, yet I felt it was a tearful defiance, a shell that would crack easily if pressure were applied. I know now that I was wrong on all those counts. You are not a vulnerable, misunderstood child but a bad-tempered, shrewish woman. In fact, the words you wore emblazoned across your shirt that night said it all—you are, indeed, a *bitch*!'

If he had thrown her head-first into the canal Jo could not have been more stupefied. It was a shock, she told herself, that caused a rush of hot tears to spring to her eyes, and fiercely she blinked them away, amazed by her own inconsistency. For hours she had prodded, jabbed and baited him, insult after insult had been heaped upon his head, she had sneered, taunted and reviled. Why then, now that she had managed to upset his damnable equilibrium, did she feel like a sail deprived of wind? Like a cockleshell boat left to the mercy of the elements?

Then temper flared. How dared this impoverished *conte*, this unscrupulous merchant, take exception to anything she said or did?

'Very well, *signore*,' she hissed, 'now that you've arrived at a true assessment of my worth, can I take it you no longer wish to hold me to my promise? That the marriage will not now take place?'

With one elbow resting on the parapet of the bridge he carelessly but thoroughly scrutinised her. 'It most certainly will,' he finally decided, 'everything will go ahead as planned.'

She turned her head away to hide her expression. Disappointment had brought a lump to her throat; she had convinced herself that this man's will would easily crack; he had seemed to bend in which ever direction she desired, yet instead of snapping he rebounded, sometimes painfully, like a steel spring. Much more venom would be needed if she were to rout this beast of prey!

They lunched in a small *ristorante* with an unpretentious frontage consisting of cracked walls, arched windows and hollowed stone steps leading down into a cellar-like room spaced out with very functional tables laid with spotless white linen reaching down to the level of spartan wooden chairs.

Leo seemed well known to the proprietor, who greeted him with outflung arms and a stream of rapid words in a dialect Jo could not understand. When they were seated Leo waved away the menu and order. '*Fegato alla veneziana* and a bottle of Bordolino, if you please, Pietro.'

In response to her raised eyebrows he explained. 'Calves' liver fried with onions is an experience you must not miss. I think you will enjoy it, but,' his tone became dry, 'if you do not then I'm sure Pietro could supply you with some English fish and chips.'

'I rarely eat fish and chips,' she replied coldly, resentful of the implication that she had no palate for good food.

'Excellent, then perhaps we are on the verge of discovering one thing at least about which we will not disagree.'

They ate in silence, Leo seemingly preoccupied yet solicitous enough to remember to replenish her glass whenever necessary, and Jo, ravenously appreciative of the food placed before her yet too stiff-necked to put her apreciation into words.

His good humour seemed completely restored by the time they had finished their meal. In an indulgent tone he questioned, 'Your father tells me you have visited your grandmother frequently over the years. If that is the case why have you omitted a sightseeing tour of the city before today?'

'We have always stayed with Nònna Domini in Murano. I love it there,' she confided, made mellow

49

with wine, 'although Papà and Sara often visited Venice I found Murano so fascinating they could never drag me away.'

'Your grandfather was a glassblower, I believe?'

'Yes,' she retorted sharply, immediately on the defensive.

'An honourable profession,' he soothed, sensing that she suspected him of patronage. 'Glassmaking has always been based on certain important technical secrets which have been carefully preserved among members of glassmaking families. Close co-operation between the members of a working team is vital to successful glassmaking and as this was most easily assured within a family group, fathers handed down their knowledge only to their sons who in turn instructed their sons. As a matter of fact, during the fifteenth century a law was passed ordering that no one should teach glassmaking to anyone whose father had not known the art.'

'There is nothing you can tell me about the industry, *signore*, I have studied the subject thoroughly. Did you know that French glassmakers rated the same privileges as the nobility? Freedom from taxes, for example, and the right to live in manorial style. The aristocrats of Venice, on the other hand, did not become landowners until the sixteenth century and during that period they laid down rules which were designed to protect their class from contamination; strict taboos were enforced to ensure no marriage could take place between members of the nobility and commoners, yet,' her chin lifted, green eyes sparkling with pride as they glared at him across the width of the table, 'among those whom sons of the noble families could marry without losing their rank were glass-makers' daughters!'

'And quite rightly so.' He toyed with a remnant of cheese left on his plate, suppressing a smile before continuing gallantly, 'As Venice has declined so, too, has the status of her nobility. As a member of that maligned class, I would like to put on record that I feel proud and honoured to have been chosen as a husband by a glassmaker's granddaughter.'

Chosen! Jo could have argued that the blame for that error lay with her impulsive nature, or that it had been a bluff that had rebounded, yet nothing could alter the fact that it had been she who had done the asking.

Humiliation almost choked her, but as she preceded him out of the restaurant she managed to toss across her shoulder the caustic comment,

'Try not to mind too much that your city has become a pawn shop, *signore*. As Napoleon put it: *"Dust and ashes, dead and done with, Venice spent what Venice earned"*. However, she does not sell her heirlooms cheap—be grateful that Papà could afford you!'

CHAPTER FIVE

SIGNORA MARVESE, Vincente's mother, was a fiercely-fond example of Italian matriarch. No woman in the world, in her eyes, was worthy of the great honour of becoming wife to her son. But she was prepared to tolerate Sara, who was dainty, feminine, and satisfyingly *pliable*. Also she possessed one redeeming feature—a rich father.

Jo, on the other hand, she found quite incompatible. The girl was rude, overbearing, shockingly outspoken and showed no deference whatsoever towards Leonardo, her intended husband, nor indeed towards any member of his family. Her prim mouth set as, glancing across the dinner-table, she watched the future Contessa stabbing morosely with her fork a delicious slice of veal that had been beaten thin, coated with breadcrumbs, then delicately browned in butter.

'The dish is not to your liking, *signorina?*' she enquired, her displeasure thinly veiled.

Jo's hand jerked up and the Signora's breath caught as, held by a clear emerald gaze, she had to concede that at times the girl was extraordinarily beautiful.

'What ...?' The rudely spoken word caused the Signora to revise her opinion—the girl was impossible, her nephew Leonardo must be out of his mind!

'Forgive my daughter's absorption with her own affairs, *signora*,' Jo's father apologised smoothly. 'Her mind is no doubt churning with thoughts of clothes and flowers and wedding bells.'

When Jo scowled at him he threw a glance that warned: 'Behave—or else!' before resuming his smoothing of the Signora's feathers.

'Your wife was English, Signore Domini, was she not?' Vincente's mother enquired. 'A cool, distant race, I've always thought, with characteristics completely opposite to your own. You must share with my nephew your formula for successfully managing a wayward temperament. Sara here,' she cast her an indulgent glance, 'will cause my son no misgivings, I feel sure, but her sister, it seems to me, possesses all the independence of her mother's race. You will have your work cut out, Leo,' she wagged a plump, beringed finger in his direction, 'to train her into obedient ways.'

'I'm not a performing seal!' Jo cast such a withering look the Signora's playful expression immediately froze.

'Nor do I fancy the role of animal trainer, Zia,' Leo reproved his aunt. 'In common with most Italians you tend to compare English girls unfavourably with those of your own race. You are very misguided. The English have a saying—so well used the truth of it must have been proven over the years— "Do not judge a book by its cover." Jo's cover,' he smiled across at her, 'may seem hard and unbending, but I can assure you that I find myself becoming more and more engrossed as I turn each page.'

'Yuk!' Jo's utterance of disgust was so loud it brought colour rushing to Sara's cheeks and a steely glint into her father's eyes. 'The delusions which mislead men arise from their tendency to believe that to be true which corresponds to their wishes!'

Leo's lips twitched as he saw utter bewilderment clouding his aunt's face, then the frown as she tried to make sense of the ponderous sentence. Even Jo's father was perplexed, uncertain whether or not his tempestuous daughter had once again insulted their host. Kindly, Leo helped them out.

'Jo's argument is sound, but because it deals with a matter upon which she feels strongly she has fallen into the trap of concealing her point behind superfluous words. Reduced to its simplest form, what I'm sure she meant is that men's thought processes tend to run on the following lines:

All cats are four-legged animals
Fido is a four-legged animal
Therefore Fido is a cat.

In other words, she is telling me that the conclusion I have drawn could just as easily be false.'

'Then why didn't she say so in the first place!' Jo's father snapped, made to feel foolish by his daughter's irritating habit of flaunting her intelligence, an annoying trait she quite often employed in order to prove that she was as good as any man. Why, he pondered wearily, looking across at Sara who was happily holding hands with Vincente under the table, could I not have been blessed with *two* gentle, accommodating daughters? What have I done to deserve a virago like Jo who can look so appealing but who is constantly at war with herself as well as with most members of the opposite sex?

Sensitive to his feelings of inadequacy, the Signora stood up, signalling to the two girls. 'Shall we take coffee in the *salotto* and leave these men in peace to sip their port and smoke their cigars?'

To her scandalised amazement, Jo folded her arms across her chest and wriggled back into her chair. 'I'm staying here. I like port and I'm not at all averse to a cigar now and again.'

'*Jo!*' Her father's voice thundered through the room. She opened her mouth to argue her right to stay, marshalling all the verbal thrusts that had cut to and fro across the Students' Hall during debates on women's equality, but just as she was about to launch into speech she noticed, out of the corner of her eye, a figure with head bent and shoulders heaving as he tried unsuccessfully to hide the fact that he was convulsed with laughter. Her fury turned on him, the annoyance caused by her father a mere pin-prick in comparison to the rage aroused by the man she was being forced to marry.

'Shut up! Don't you dare laugh at me!' Her fists clenched, fingers itching to scratch the length of brown cheeks as, completely helpless, Leo clutched his sides, swept along on a paroxysm of mirth. 'You ... you ... *conceited, chauvinistic pig!*' She ground her heel into the carpet. 'Damn you! I don't know why I even bother to try ...!' She swept from the room, head proudly poised, eyes flashing resentment, and ground her teeth when two other masculine voices joined Leo's in a demoralising, humorous chorus.

She had been in her bedroom only a few minutes when Sara, flustered and visibly anxious, followed her inside. Wide-eyed, she watched Jo struggling out of her evening dress, a delicate confection of pale green cotton that had lent to her the charm of a woodland nymph, and gasped a protest when it was flung on to the floor and trampled under Jo's angry feet.

'Jo, what are you doing? You're surely not going to bed already? Signora Marvese has sent me to fetch you; there is something very important she wishes to discuss.'

Jo grabbed a denim skirt from out of her wardrobe and began rummaging in a drawer for a matching top. 'I don't doubt she has,' she gritted, 'but I have no intention of sitting with hands primly folded while she lectures me on my faults and outlines the sort of behaviour expected of a future *contessa*. You can go back and tell the old ragbag to get lost—I'm going out!'

'Out?' Sara repeated stupidly, ignoring the insult to her future mother-in-law. 'But you can't, not without an escort—it simply isn't done. The Signora will be scandalised, and as for Leo ...'

'Oh, for heaven's sake!' Jo turned on her such a look of exasperation Sara shivelled. 'I declare, Sara, the longer you stay in this country the more orientated you become! You're like a snail which for years has been unattached from its shell and now that it's found it has curled into a complacent ball, determined never again to budge! At home in England you and I have gone wherever we wished whenever we wished, sometimes together and sometimes alone. Mere weeks ago the idea of being confined to the house because an escort was not available would have reduced you to hysterical laughter, yet now you're implying that we should embrace attitudes that were rejected by Englishwomen over a century ago. Well, you may be willing to be brainwashed, but I am not! I'm going out now and I'm going alone. If the Signora doesn't like it then she just might, given a bit of luck, persuade her stiff-necked nephew to think twice about holding me to a promise given under duress.'

Experiencing a sense of freedom that was amazing considering her modern upbringing, Jo hurried from the *palazzo* and in no time at all was swallowed into a maze of alleyways, archways and winding passages running through dismal back streets, then disgorging with pleasant suddenness into busy spacious squares. Giving no thought as to how she was to find her way back, she followed her nose, tramping along wide, airy quaysides, down ancient lanes, along paved alleyways, then slowed to a saunter when she recognised in the distance the Rialto bridge Leo had pointed out with pride that morning. She crossed its crooked hump and was immediately surrounded by a noisy, picturesque marketplace, then lost all track of time as she enjoyed the banter being exchanged by market traders, examined gilded ornaments, St Christopher medallions, admired stalls piled high with strings of onions, casually-heaped lettuce, glowing apples, sliced coconut, oranges sliced before her eyes and then offered in succulent portions to tempt her to buy.

With a sticky trail of juice trickling down her chin, she paused before a display of carnations and was hurriedly besieged by an enthusiastic flower-seller with a patter so persuasive she finally staggered away clutching an armful of the cloying, heavily perfumed flowers. The strap of her sandal was chafing her heel, so thankfully she limped towards an outdoor café, collapsed into a chair and deposited her fragrant burden on to a small metal table.

'*Caffe, per favore*,' she begged of the hovering waiter, then kicked off her sandals preparing to enjoy the sights around her. She was just finishing her coffee when across the rim of her cup she caught a glimpse of bold eyes fastened upon her face before her glance slid away. The obviously admiring Venetian caused her no qualms. Nuisances such as he, she had discovered from past experience, usually shrivelled when at the receiving end of a frozen stare.

To her annoyance her admirer, impelled by boundless conceit, moved his chair closer, leaving mere inches of space between thm.

'*Buona notte, signorina*.' A fulsome smile revealed rows of teeth so white and perfect she felt an urge to poke her fist into his mouth, thereby loosening a couple of what he obviously thought were his greatest assets.

'Go away! *Andare via!*' She dismissed him with a wave of her hand.

'Ah, *inglése!*' he beamed, as delighted as if he had found a pot of gold. 'I speak English good,' he slowly enunciated, baring his tombstone teeth. Impudently he pushed aside her empty cup. 'I like English girls very much,' he confided. 'Let us share a bottle of wine.'

'No, thank you,' she treated him to a frigid stare. 'If you don't mind, I'll just continue to sit here and admire the view—*alone!*'

His toothy smile did not slip. Jo sighed. Regrettably, the reputation of English girls abroad was not good, and though she was irresistibly tempted to defend her counterparts by explaining in very concise terms the difference between liberation and immorality, she did not intend to become drawn into conversation with this pompous nuisance who, given an inch, would take the proverbial yard. So she bit her lip, her stony stare reducing his importance to that of a fly upon the wall. But then, to her great aggravation, he inched forward until their chairs were touching and hissed on a garlic-laden breath, 'You like to dance? I know of a place near here ...'

'Go and jump in the canal!' Crossly she slipped on her sandals and stood up to leave, turning her back upon the man whose persistence was infuriating. Incredibly, as she bent forward to scoop up her flowers, she felt the fleshy part of her thigh being pinched between two fingers—an old Italian

59

custom which in other circumstances she might have laughed off but which, in this instance, escalated her fiery temper beyond control. Fury added strength to her arm as she swung her heavy handbag at his head. The impact knocked him clean off his chair and as he lay sprawling on the pavement his expression of ludicrous astonishment was so funny she just had to laugh.

The events that followed were like a scene from some farcical foreign film. Jo thought later when given time to reflect. As the amorous Venetian writhed at her feet, howling with pretended pain, an enormously stout woman, gasping and wheezing in her haste, emerged from the interior of the café brandishing a large wooden spoon in Jo's direction. Patrons of the café, obviously very partisan, spilled out in her wake and in seconds she was surrounded by a hostile gesticulating mob whose sympathies, she was left in no doubt, lay with the proprietress and the man on the ground whom she had stooped to comfort. One quick glance was sufficient to confirm Jo's suspicion that he was the stout woman's son, and her heart sank.

Above the screaming tirade of abuse being directed towards her, she heard a whistle blow, then the crowd parted to admit one of the strutting, ridiculously dressed *carabinièri* whose eyes, beneath a cocked hat, gleamed cold as the sword hilt supporting his huge fist. To Jo's disgust he waved her silent and listened carefully to everything the voluble proprietress had to say, then, ignoring her own heated protests that the charges being laid against her were highly inflated, began writing in his notebook.

She lost her cool when his hand descended upon her shoulder and she began to shout, feeling prickings of genuine fear. 'The woman is mad! I had no intention of murdering her son—I was merely defending myself. In fact, if in England he had attempted the same impertinent action I could have quite easily had him arrested and charged with indecent assault. Look, I can prove what he did!' Forgetful of Italian modesty, she hitched up her skirt to search for the beginnings of a bruise she felt certain had appeared on her thigh. Gasps of horror from the watching women and jeers from the men recalled her sanity as, feeling shame out of all proportion to her crime, she hastily covered up the pulsating bruise.

'You will come with me, *signorina*.' The policeman's voice echoed with distaste. 'I am charging you with violence and with offending public morality. Do not try to argue,' he placed a hand as big as a palm leaf upon her shoulder and began pushing her before him. 'You English girls are a nuisance, you tempt our sons, unsettle our daughters and outrage our parents with your immoral ways. If I had my way you would all be banned from our shores, but as it is,' he shrugged regretfully, 'I am only authorised to lock you away.'

It could not be happening! she thought frantically, not really *happening*. She must actually be experiencing a nightmare, one so realistic she could feel the waves of the Grand Canal rocking the speeding police boat and actually feel the sword, buckled around the waist of the musical comedy figure sitting next to her, digging into her leg. The breeze seemed real enough as it rushed through her hair, as did the stars twinkling in a midnight blue sky, also lights strung out along the canal, their reflection decorating the water with an endless jewelled fringe.

The stern-faced man seated behind a desk in the police station was too down-to-earth to be other than human. He committed to writing all the lies that had been told about Jo, then, without even lifting his head, waved her out of sight. Roughly she was escorted along a dank passageway, down a flight of stone steps, then pushed inside a dimly-lit room that would have fitted inside one of the cupboards housed within the *palazzo*.

The cold, comfortless cell, the hard mattress, the leaden pillow, were all very real. She slumped down upon the bunk and leant sideways so that her burning forehead was in contact with bars of cold steel and thought, not of her enraged father, her scandalised sister and outraged future in-laws, but of the calm, unflappable Conte, desperately wishing that —just this once—he was by her side.

'Oh, Jo girl, you've done it this time!' she squeezed the whisper past the lump in her throat. 'There'll be hell to pay!'

CHAPTER SIX

At five o'clock the following morning Jo was given a bowl of water, a coarse grey square of towelling and an offensively-smelling sliver of soap. Shuddering her disgust, she dabbed water over her face and bathed eyes that felt gritty with lack of sleep. After patting her face dry, she combed her hair through with shaking fingers, wishing she had thought to retrieve her comb from the handbag the police had taken into their custody the previous evening.

The wash refreshed her. She sat on the edge of the bunk feeling hungry but at the same time nauseated, which was just as well, because when breakfast arrived she took one look at the metal bowl containing some unrecognisable brown mess and pushed it aside. For ages, it seemed, she sat watching the sun moving gradually from the lip of a window situated high, just beneath the level of the ceiling, until it disappeared from sight leaving the cell once more dank and grim. She shivered, dejection washing over her. The grim-faced policemen had refused to listen when she had begged to be allowed to contact her father. Back at the *palazzo* they were bound to be worrying—after all, to go out alone for a short while was one thing, but to stay out all night was quite another.

Her mind raced, filling in the time by preparing

the long and complicated explanation that was bound to be demanded of her. She had no idea of the time, but a further meal had been offered and rejected before she heard the rattling of keys, urgent footsteps, and a resonant voice, strange in tone as it snapped an order to some unfortunate offender, yet hearteningly familiar.

She jumped to her feet and stumbled forward, so that the sight that confronted Leo as he approached the cell was that of a small, frightened figure caged behind bars, with eyes that seemed enormous staring out of a pinched, ashen face.

'*Dannazióne!*' He allowed himself the luxury of one expletive as he waited, savagely controlled, until the guard's fumbling fingers had turned the massive key, then as the cell door was flung open he opened his arms to receive her.

To Jo, at the moment, it seemed the most natural thing in the world to fly through the cell door and bury her head deep into his shoulder. She heaved a great shudder of relief and Leo's arms tightened into a protective circle, his lips brushing her brow as he murmured tender, soothing phrases. He comforted her until she had stopped trembling, then, keeping her pressed to his side, he guided her along the passageway, up the stairs and into the glaring brightness of the police station's main office.

There seemed to be a great deal of commotion, many hurrying footsteps, many voices raised in voluble argument, but Jo kept her face pressed into Leo's shoulder, ashamed of weak tears that had welled into her eyes.

An authoritative voice, tinged with bluster, began protesting, '*Signore*, how were we to know? The girl was wandering the streets alone, late at night. She caused a commotion in a local café and we were sent for—what were we to think? We had no alternative but to arrest her!'

It was typical of Leo that he did not raise his voice. Leo—the lion who never roared, the beast without a bite.

'Enough!' he silenced them coldly. 'I will return later.'

Even Jo sensed the anger contained within the few quietly bitten words and was moved to feel a stirring of sympathy for the men who fell into an uncomfortable silence broken only by the shuffling of feet and a gruff, embarrassed cough.

As he handed her into the speedboat and ascertained that she was comfortable before taking over the controls she chanced a glance at his profile. His lips were a stern, straight line, compressed as if to stem words he could not trust himself to speak. His face, taut as a mask, had a hint of greyness beneath its tan and his eyes, lashed thick and black, looked haggard devoid of their golden gleam, dulled with searching through a long and worrying night.

Once back at the *palazzo* he again took command. As soon as she stepped into the main hall her father, Sara, Vincente and his mother descended upon her, firing rapid questions, barely waiting for her stumbling answers before asking yet another.

'Jo, what on earth happened?'

'Jo, where have you been?'

'Where, may I ask, did you spend the night, *signorina*?'

'Why didn't you send a message, Sara was frantic with worry!'

In response to the bell Leo had pressed a maid-servant appeared.

'Maria, take the *signorina* up to her room, see that she has a hot bath, something light to eat and is left undisturbed for the rest of the day.'

'But, Leo!' Sara protested, 'we must know——'

'Your sister is in no state to answer questions just now. This evening, if she feels inclined, she can satisfy your curiosity, but until then I insist she is left in peace to recover from her experience. Go now with Maria,' he instructed Jo. Then more kindly, 'If you feel well enough you may join us for dinner this evening.'

For once it was a great relief to do as she was told. Her head was aching, eyelids would not be willed to stay open over heavy eyes. She felt unclean, and stepped eagerly into the bath Maria had prepared, then afterwards, warm, dry, and smelling sweetly of talc, she climbed into the huge four-poster and was asleep before Maria had tucked the bedcovers around her.

Hours later she stirred, opened her eyes, then, with a long, luxurious yawn, rolled over on to her back.

'Ah, at last you have come back to us, *nipotina*!'

'Nònna Domini!' Jo turned dazed eyes upon the figure seated in a chair drawn close to the bed-side. 'Whatever are you doing here?'

'I was brought here early this morning by your very charming *fidanzato*!'

'My betrothed ...? Oh, you mean the Conte!'

'Naturally,' the old lady spoke severely, 'is he not the one you have chosen to wed?'

'Well ... er ...' Jo struggled upright, then, deciding the subject needed more thought, she dodged the issue. 'But I don't understand, Nònna, why he found it necessary to bring you here.'

Her grandmother was small, slender, with a sweet expression and a mouth that could adopt very determined lines when occasionally she felt inclined to be stubborn. 'When he told me that you were missing I asked if I might return here with him. In the early hours he came to my house. Seemingly, all during the night he had explored every avenue in search of you and I was his last resort. His disappointment was great when I told him I had not seen you, but even then, at a time of great personal anxiety, he was courteous enough to apologise for disturbing my sleep and for being the bearer of such worrying news. He begged me to return to my bed, but when I insisted I would not rest until I knew you were safe he brought me back to the *palazzo* so that I would be near at hand when finally he discovered your whereabouts—which I had no doubt he would do,' she chuckled, at ease now that her favourite granddaughter was safe. 'You have chosen as a husband a very determined man, *nipóte*, one who would have upturned every stone in Venice had his search been much longer prolonged.'

Jo stared, the image of Leo in such a frantic state

was not an easy one to visualise. 'I think you may have misjudged him a little, Nònna. The Conte never allows himself to become agitated, he is at all times cool, unflappable—even remote.'

Her grandmother turned upon her a gimlet stare. 'Just how long have you known the Conte?'

Jo swallowed hard and began plucking at the bed-sheet with nervous fingers. Here was her chance to gain an ally. She was very fond of her grandmother and she knew the fondness was returned. Perhaps, with the aid of her wisdom, they would be able to find some way out of her predicament. 'I've known him only a few days,' she began in a rush. 'The engagement came about through a silly wager, but nevertheless the Conte insists upon holding me to my promise because he needs the marriage dowry Papà is providing.'

Her grandmother seemed not one whit disturbed. With a shrug of her thin shoulders she observed mildly, 'If such is the case, then you are indeed fortunate. Consider how you would have felt if the man with whom the wager had been made were not the young and handsome Conte Tempera but an old, ugly specimen of manhood, the sight of whom would make a young woman cringe. But then I think I do you an injustice, *nipóte*,' she chuckled at some private joke. 'It has been said that you favour your mother, but in one respect at least you are very like your father. It would be very hard, I might even say impossible, to force either of you into a situation that is not to your liking. You profess to dislike the Conte, are suspicious of his motives and

68

say you are angry about his insistence that the marriage must take place. Think deeply, child, be as honest with yourself as you are with others. Are you not secretly gratified by the fact that you have managed, albeit with seeming unwillingness, to capture the man you wanted?'

'*Nònna!*' Jo bounced out of bed and glowered down at her grandmother. 'By implication, you're reducing me to a level of silly flibbertygibbets like Sara whose sole ambition in life is to find a husband! Very much to the contrary, I'm anxious to continue with my career, the only men needed in my life are those whose brains I can pick. I'm not averse to male companionship, indeed, I enjoy it in the right place and at the right time, but marriage has no part in my plans. So you see how ridiculous is your implication that I deliberately engineered the situation that's causing me so much unhappiness!'

Nònna Domini stood up, looking unimpressed. 'Poor Jo,' she sighed, 'if only I could hold up a mirror to your soul! I feel so sorry for the young girls of today who live in a world which does its best, night and day, to change the nature of woman, to strip her of her femininity, to convince her that wedlock is a padlock, to argue against our sex's most natural instinct—that of bearing children. You must fight against such insidious propaganda, Jo, if you are ever to discover your true self. Otherwise you will starve—not from lack of bread but from lack of love.'

Her grandmother, Jo decided, once she had been left alone to dress, was old and pitifully out of touch with modern-day life. She shrugged slim shoulders into a strapless black dress, low-cut at the front and plunging deeply at the back, held in position by sheer will power and the genius of a cutter who had measured, cut, snipped and tucked the material in order to obtain the maximum adhesion using the minimum of support—a dress which demanded the utmost sangfroid of its wearer and culled gasps of admiration, willing and unwilling, from wondering observers. Each time she had worn it she had asked herself: will it stay put. It always had. The hypnotic effect of smooth, unblemished shoulders and milk-white curve of breast, half hidden, half displayed by a flimsy film of net, was sensational. Tonight she felt she needed the boost the dress would give her. Anxiety about her welfare had had time to wane; if the going should get tough she would need all the armour the outfit would provide.

She was putting finishing touches to her hair when Sara entered her room. As Jo turned from the mirror Sara's frown was very much in evidence. 'Oh, no, Jo, you're not in an "I dare anything" mood again!'

'I don't know what you mean.' Calmly Jo swung round to the mirror, allowing Sara the full benefit of a back bared to well below the waist with, out-standing against one shoulder blade, a black, circular mole, perfectly placed. 'A devil's kiss,' her mother had once laughingly proclaimed it, much to Jo's delight and Sara's trepidation.

'Something gets into you whenever you wear that dress,' she frowned, 'you take such delight in shocking people.' Her rather censorious tone changed to a plea. 'Please, Jo, try to behave tonight. Papà is already very angry with you, Signora Marvese and Vincente have both been shocked and bewildered by your actions, whereas Leo ...'

'Yes ...?' Jo swung round to challenge her sister. 'Tell me about Leo, is he, too, shocked, angry and ashamed? I must admit he didn't seem to be when he delivered me from jail this morning, but then he's too much of a gentleman to show his displeasure to a lady in distress. Tell me what you think, Sara. Did last night's escapade do the trick, has Signora Marvese finally managed to persuade the Conte that as a Tempera bride I leave much to be desired? Come, tell me what harsh words were bandied about during my absence.'

Jo was expecting a spirited reply from her usually voluble sister, but to her surprise Sara did not react as expected. She stood in dejected silence, her bottom lip quivering, then in a gesture of utter hopelessness crumpled, a tight ball of misery, on to Jo's bed and began to sob. Jo started towards her, sensing that this time Sara was not acting, that her tears were tears of real despair. 'Sara, what's wrong?' She shook her by the shoulder. 'Were you so worried about me? I'm sorry I caused you all so much concern. I didn't mean——'

Sara's head jerked up, an expression of unmistakable dislike on her tear-streaked face. '*You* are sorry!' she choked. 'You're not half so sorry as I—sorry that my happiness is in the hands of a person such as you, sorry that you have the power to destroy my life, sorry that instead of a sister with my well-being at heart I have one who's selfish, stubborn, concerned about fulfilling her own desires even if she wrecks my life in the process!'

Jo sank down beside her. She was used to such recriminations, but this time Sara was not railing against what might happen but what already had happened. 'Tell me about it,' she demanded crisply, knowing soothing words and denials would be useless.

Sara gulped, then rolled on her back, staring at the canopy above the bed as if on its lace-patterned surface she could see projected an image of the scene that had occurred the night before. 'When you ran out of the *palazzo* last night Signora Marvese went in search of Leo demanding that he should follow you and fetch you back. To everyone's surprise he seemed unperturbed, merely shrugging and making some oblique remark about a kitten pent up becoming a tiger which we did not understand but which seemed to satisfy Papà, because he, too, made no further objection. For an hour or so we played cards. Your name was never mentioned, yet your absence hung over the room like a cloud. Then finally, when it was midnight and you'd still not returned, the Signora could contain her anger no longer and began to rant and rave, demanding of Leo that he should call off the wedding, saying you were not fit to be his bride and that your actions would bring disgrace upon his name. By that time I could tell that Leo, too, was worried, but he made no reply, just brushed her aside as he strode out of the *palazzo* to begin his search. This incensed the Signora so greatly she turned on Papà. It was terrible, Jo!' She sat upright, gulped back a quivering sob and with eyes mirroring the extent of her misery continued reliving the nightmare.

'Her remarks became outrageous, too outrageous for Papà to endure. It was when she accused you of being morally lax that he lost his temper and they began to row in earnest. Vincente and I tried to intervene, but we were shouted down. After many bitter exchanges, the Signora incensed Papà almost to the point of apoplexy by declaring that the late Conte, Leo's father, would turn in his grave at the idea of his son marrying someone as unworthy as yourself. "If one of my daughters is not fit to be accepted by the Tempera family, *signora*," he exploded, "then neither is the other! That being the case, the marriage between Sara and your son will not now take place—I here and now formally withdraw my permission!"'

'Oh, glory ...!' Jo's breathed explanation was drowned by a further outburst of sobbing from Sara. Both of them knew how impossible it could be to change their father's mind once he had come to a decision. The future for Sara seemed bleak.

Jo left her sobbing on the bed and began pacing the room. Something drastic would have to be done. Although she held no brief for Vincente, whom she considered to be a weak and vacillating character completely under his mother's thumb, to Sara he represented all she wanted from life. Sara, too, possessed her share of Domini single-mindedness.

She had set her heart upon becoming Vincente's wife and was liable, if thwarted, to become a creature of unbearable moods and depressions.

'And it will be all your fault,' Jo told herself gloomily, searching her mind for a solution.

There was only one—time and time again her mind shied away from it, but finally it had to be faced. She would have to go through with her marriage to the Conte, it was the only way her father's ruffled feathers could be smoothed. Signora Marvese could not influence Leo as she did her son, so her dissenting voice would quickly be silenced.

Jo's fists clenched as she fought the influence of an inner voice crying out against the forfeiture of freedom, against the coercion of being forced to marry when marriage was the last thing she had intended, against the wrench of being deprived of a career whose challenge she would have enjoyed, especially when she would have become one of a small female minority within a male-dominated sphere. But she owed a duty to her sister—she would have to fulfil that duty and leave the rest to the gods. If the Conte was still interested in obtaining a bargain bride then let the sale be finalised!

She sought him out, anxious to test his reaction to the decision that had been made, her pale, subdued face quaintly at odds with her flamboyant outfit. He was pouring out pre-dinner drinks and when she stepped inside the *salotto* he looked up and saw her image reflected in the mirror directly facing him. Their eyes collided through glass and for a second she felt startled by the golden, alert gleam that traced her reflection, lingering longer than was polite upon smooth, curving shoulders outstanding stark as alabaster against a density of filmy black bodice. She tensed, expecting censure, but he turned to face her wearing his usual expression of urbanity to observe.

'You are not wearing your locket. It would look well with that dress.'

'I don't agree.' She stepped farther into the room, projecting bravado, yet feeling an annoying quirking at the knees. 'You Venetians have an unfortunate tendency to paint the lily. We English, on the other hand, consider simplicity has more impact.'

'Beauty needs no adornment, eh?' Without consulting her wishes, he handed her a glass of pale golden sherry. 'In this instance I will not argue with that.' As Jo accepted the proffered glass she blushed, made to feel naked as his slow, interested glance slid along a slope of shoulder, down a curvaceous breast, then plunged to linger among tantalising shadows cast by net enthralling, mysterious as midnight.

'I've come to apologise.' Fiercely she suppressed the tremor in her voice as, casually turning aside, she exposed the devil's kiss startling against a white expanse of shoulder, to his interested gaze.

'This time, *cara*, I consider an apology is justified. Last night I suffered some very anxious hours.'

She swung round, puzzled by a voice that had sounded strangulated, then decided she had been mistaken as she searched a face impassively unreadable.

'Yes,' she jerked, struggling with a surge of depression. 'Sara has just been telling me about the row and I want to do all I can to patch things up between Signora Marvese and my father. But before I do so, you must let me tell you the true details concerning last night's fiasco. The police wouldn't listen to anything I tried to say, but I'm sure you will give me a fair hearing.' She drew in a deep breath and without giving herself the time to wonder why it was so important that he should believe her, launched into her explanation.

Leo heard her out in silence, one arm draped casually across the shelf of a fireplace sculpted from black marble, the other occupied with a goblet of fine crystal, twirling the stem within sensitive brown fingers as, with dark head bowed, he paid rapt attention to its swirling contents. Giving him no time to interrupt, Jo spoke in a tumbled rush, watching for any change of expression, however slight, upon the regal profile etched with cameo clarity against a background of black stone.

His lips quirked once when, her voice raised in indignation, she recounted the flesh-pinching episode, but he let it pass without comment, continuing his mood of sombre contemplation until, her explanation finished, she began with disjointed phrases to outline her remedy for undoing the harm her actions had caused.

'It seems I now have no alternative but to marry you—my first duty must be towards Sara. Your aunt, I'm sure, must already be regretting her thoughtless remarks, but Papà will not be easily mollified. So if I can somehow convince him that I really *do* want to marry you then I'm sure he'll raise no objection. Our marriage will remove every obstacle threatening Sara's happiness.'

Leo jerked upright, spearing her with a look of glacial displeasure. 'Forgive my obtuseness, but I had formed the impression that you had already promised to become my wife. Arrangements for our wedding have been in process for some days, yet you speak as if only this minute you have reached a final decision?'

Jo cast him an uneasy glance, suspicious of a calm that seemed cast like oil over turbulent emotions. With a nervous shrug she crossed over to the window before attempting an explanation. 'I know I promised to marry you,' she gulped, 'but I somehow never really expected to have to carry out that promise. To me, the situation has always seemed unreal, as unreal as Venice itself, a ruined city full of relics, a museum wherein antiquated customs have to be brushed aside like the cobwebs one keeps brushing from one's face and from out of one's hair. A city peopled with beings living in the mediaeval past, women who revel in servitude and men with attitudes to match. Can you blame me,' she appealed desperately, 'after living the sort of life I've lived, for thinking I'd stepped into some kind of fairy tale, an Alice in Wonderland dream inhabited by unbelievable creatures that would disappear the moment I woke up?'

He moved with lithe, cat-like tread, demolishing the width of the room in the time it took her to draw breath. She would not have believed his grip could be so cruel, fingers that dug into the soft flesh of her shoulders, flexing hard, gouging a depth of unbearable pain. He was very angry, she realised, as he released his grip upon her shoulder to enclose her slender neck within one hand, at the same time fastening the other upon her waist to jerk her forward against his chest. Her terrified eyes caught his expression as his head lowered, the glitter of eyes flashing cold fury, nostrils flaring wide, a savagely resentful mouth intent upon punishment.

He kissed her only once, a kiss of long duration that began chilling as steel against steel, then gradually, as metal melts, developing a relaxing warmth that rose to bearable heat, then progressed into scorching flame that erupted ultimately into a frightening flare of passion. No devil's kiss could have inflicted a more searing impression than his. She felt marked for life, not unobtrusively like the mole crushed beneath his hand, but blatantly, so that the whole world would look at her and know that she was his.

He released her so suddenly she sagged against him, her red head, dejected as a broken match, supported by his comfortless shoulder. As if from miles away his voice resounded, suave, composed, echoing none of the passion they had shared.

'Nothing becomes real until it is experienced, *bambina*. I regret having had to waken a dreamer, but I could not allow you to enter into marriage with a man you look upon as a shadow. I'm human, *tesora mia*, as are you; together we will find love in marriage.'

'*Love!*' Joe choked out the hateful word. 'Love could never usurp the loathing I feel for you!'

He shrugged. 'Love, hate, they are both qualities of passion. At least you have said goodbye for ever to your limbo of illusion. Perhaps now, having been shaken from your cradle of indifference, you will really begin to feel.'

Jo's blood ran cold as she stared into the face of a stranger. A lion without a roar, she had labelled him, a beast without bite. The menace of the jungle was all around him—how could she have failed to see, how could she have forgotten that of all God's creatures there is but one that cannot be made the slave of the lash—the cat, the family with the lion at its head!

CHAPTER SEVEN

THEIR wedding day dawned bright and golden. As Jo stepped outside the *palazzo* on her father's arm everything seemed to be glittering, as if artists had mingled sparkling wine into their paints or fairies had waved their wands over buildings, dusting them with diamonds.

The Conte's crested gondola was bobbing at its mooring post and as she stepped inside a steadying hand was offered by one of the menservants dressed for his role of gondolier in a splendid pink uniform. He looked slightly self-conscious, Jo thought, as carefully he arranged her veil over velvet cushions. Signora Marvese had demanded a ceremony worthy of the house of Tempera. In the old days, she had insisted, Venetian brides had been celebrated throughout Europe for the magnificence of their clothes and the grandeur of their weddings. So the city's leading coiffeur had dressed Jo's hair, had shampooed, snipped and brushed until it resembled a length of red-gold silk. The front was combed severely back to accommodate the wreath of golden leaves worn by Tempera brides and the rest, entwined with golden thread, had been fashioned into a scroll that rested low on the nape of her neck. Her shoulders were bare and her dress, borrowed from legions of previous brides, had a full skirt, a nipped-in waist, and was fashioned out of priceless silk damask woven with golden threads.

A crowd of sightseers had gathered outside the *palazzo* hoping for a sight of the bride. As Jo waited for her father to join her a breeze lifted her veil, exposing white, set features, a firmly disciplined mouth, and eyes mirroring a depth of uncertainty. Oohs and aahs of satisfaction came from the watching women—it was as it should be; the Conte's young English bride, though reputedly headstrong, was nevertheless conscious of the honour about to be bestowed upon her.

With a fluttering of pink satin ribbons the gondola set off towards the church with, following in its wake, a trail of motorboats transporting the wedding guests. The church was not far from the *palazzo* but, although all traffic on the canal gave way to the gondola with much blaring of horns and goodnatured badinage, the journey, to Jo, seemed interminable. She schooled herself to return friendly waves and to smile her appreciation of good wishes being yelled by spectators lining the canal, but her heart grew heavier by the minute until, when finally the gondola drew up in front of the church and a priest, at once beaming and benevolent, advanced to greet her, she felt her body was encasing a leaden weight.

Leo, looking indescribably distinguished in a morning suit, was waiting inside the church, the interior of which, as she walked down the aisle towards him, was merely a blurred impression of wooden-beamed ceiling, tall arcades, painted cherubs, and a scent that seemed the very essence of mediaeval Venice, a mixture of flowers and Oriental spices that caught in her throat, causing her to choke on her responses.

Surprisingly, she had become too numbed over the past weeks to argue her dislike of the vow to obey. Her own lethargy surprised her. She felt she had been sapped of the will to fight, as if the combined pressures of Leo, Vincente, the Signora, Sara and her father had bludgeoned her spirit, reducing the scratching kitten to a bleating lamb.

When the Conte slipped a heavy gold ring upon her finger she gasped and involuntarily jerked her hand away. But Leo was prepared for such reaction and grasped her firmly by the wrist while the ring was slid into place. Then it was all over. She and the Conte were man and wife—choirboys were singing of it; an organ was joyously pealing a hymn in praise of it; guests were laughing and chatting of it, and the priest, beaming and rotund, seemed enormously proud of the part he had played in sentencing her to a lifetime of bondage.

Leo lowered his head and before she could dodge out of the way brushed her cold lips with his own.

'*Che duri per sempre, cara,*' he murmured, holding her still.

May it last for ever!

'Not if I can help it!' she hissed in a most unbridelike tone. His eyebrows shot up, then with a small smile of reproof that set her teeth on edge he led her up the aisle, out of the church, and towards the beribboned bridal gondola with, on its high-necked prow, the crest of lions with cold, glittering stare.

Back at the *palazzo* a feast had been prepared, a culinary triumph masterminded by Signora Marvese, who was in her element when sufficient money could be spared to imitate the grandeur of yester-year. It was a buffet luncheon, hot and cold meals served to the guests' individual choice. White-fringed, pink-curled hams, succulent barons of beef still hot from the oven and basking in their own sizzling juices, tender chickens with crisp brown skins that crackled at a bite, huge prawns, blood-red salmon, grilled bacon rashers wrapped artistic-ally around slices of tender liver. There were innumerable side dishes, iced-sponge cakes oozing cream, crystal bowls containing a wide selection of desserts, the inevitable *lasagne* and *misto mare*, a fried pot-pourri of unbelievably delicious seafood.

'Shall I fetch you something to nibble, Jo?' Sara zoomed upon the bridal pair as they waited at the entrance of the main *salotto* to welcome stragglers. 'You must be starving,' she urged, full of concern now that she could look upon her sister as an asset rather than an obstacle. 'You wouldn't eat breakfast and also, if my memory serves me correctly, you refused supper last night. I'll get you a devil on horseback,' she coaxed in response to Jo's wave of dissent, 'that's one delicacy I've never known you to refuse.'

'Yes, please do that, Sara,' Leo accepted on Jo's

behalf, 'we shall have to remain here a few minutes longer, so by all means supply Jo with her devil on horseback.'

'Don't bother,' Jo refused coldly. 'I've had my fill of devils for one day.' As she scowled at Leo, her meaning unmistakable, Sara protested:

'How can you imply that Leo is a devil—he's too much of a gentleman!'

'According to Shelley,' Jo fixed her with a stony stare, 'sometimes the devil *is* a gentleman!'

Sara's shoulders lifted in despair. Casting Leo a sympathetic glance, she appealed of him: 'How will you tame her temper, Leo? She's already driven Papà and myself almost to despair, what remedy will you employ that we have not?'

'A soothing tongue, perhaps.' Leo's grave answer held a hint of rebuke that made Sara feel decidedly uncomfortable. The Conte could be gently cutting when he wished. For a surprised second she felt almost sorry for Jo, who had stated emphatically on more than one occasion that this descendant of the Lions of Venice was no more ferocious than a toothless tomcat. He, on the other hand, seemed very intuitive of Jo's needs—for the understanding he seemed to think her family ought to have supplied. She shrugged, deciding their characters were too complex for her simple mind, then twirled on her heel to go in search of Vincente, her pleasant, undemanding fiancé who would bring no upheaval into her placid life. How glad she was that he differed so much in nature from his cousin—the man whose imperturbability made her shiver, a man, she sensed with rare insight, who would not enjoy victory without a fight.

When the last of the guests had been greeted, leaving them free to mingle, Leo raised Jo's hand to his lips, brushing her cold fingers with a kiss.

'You have behaved very well today, *cara*. Indeed, for the past weeks you have seemed almost docile.' His smile was wry as he enquired whimsically, 'Is it possible that you have at last come to terms with the idea of having me as a husband? It would be nice,' his golden eyes flicked across her set features as if in search of encouragement, 'if our honeymoon could begin in harmony rather than in discord.'

All of her pent-up frustration was contained in the scornful look she threw his way. 'If you think that then I must be a better actress than I thought. However, if my behaviour has pleased you then it must have also met with Papà's approval, which was my sole aim. But now that we're married and Papà can't go back on his promise to allow Sara and Vincente's wedding to take place I shall revert to normal by adding one more vow to those I've already pledged today—you have my word, *signore*, that from this day onwards you will bitterly regret having taken me for a wife!'

The unshockable Conte shrugged off the threat and politely offered her his arm. 'Our guests are waiting. For the next couple of hours do please continue acting out your role of radiant bride.'

It was hard, yet Jo somehow managed to do as he had asked, mixing freely with the guests, laughing, chatting, her manners impeccable as she was introduced to members of the family she had never previously met. Carefully she noted each introduction, expecting to be confronted by Francesca, the girl whose name had teased her mind since she had heard it mentioned by Vincente in a teasing, flippant manner that had aroused Leo's anger. But the introduction never came.

She pretended it was a game, that each of Leo's relatives was an adversary who had to be charmed, and managed with such success to fool them that by the time the reception was in full swing Leo was being inundated with congratulations from envious friends.

'What an angel you have brought into the Tempera fold, Leo!' one infatuated uncle exclaimed, bemused by the beauty, wit and charm of his new niece.

'An angel with a temper, nevertheless, Uncle Nuccio,' Leo countered with a smile, sliding a fond arm around Jo's waist.

'I have always preferred temper to meekness,' his uncle approved. 'The latter I regard as a dishonest vice and the former as an honest virtue.'

'How nice of you to champion me, Uncle,' Jo cooed, stroking a seemingly possessive hand along Leo's arm to administer a vicious secret nip. It must have felt agonising, but he did not flinch. Rather white around the lips, he covered her punishing fingers with his hand, exerting crushing pressure until she released her grip, all the while continuing an urbane conversation with his uncle.

Her sparkle lasted until the last ritual was being

performed, the act of the bride and groom distributing to their guests dainty lace pouches with drawstring ribbons, decorated with minute posies of flowers, each containing a handful of sugared almonds and a small card printed with the names of the bride and groom, the place and date of their wedding. It took time, because a few pretty phrases had to be exchanged with each beaming recipient so that, by the time the last favour had been handed out, Jo felt she was dragging a heavy cloak of weariness around with her, and wondered how much longer she could maintain her artificial air of gaiety.

When she stumbled Leo's arm shot out to steady her, his keen glance noting the droop of her mouth and faint shadows beneath her eyes. He looked around for Sara, caught her eye, then indicated with a wave that she should join them. She came immediately, giving an understanding nod when Leo instructed:

'Our duty is done, we can leave now without giving offence. Most of the guests will remain for hours yet, but I've no doubt that you and your father will cope with the help of Vincente and my aunt.' His last words were phrased as a question and when Sara nodded assent he smiled approval, then suggested, 'Perhaps you will accompany Jo upstairs and help to get ready for our journey? I suspect she is feeling very tired.'

For once Jo did not argue with his judgment. She *was* feeling tired, and depressed, and apprehensive all at the same time. Blood rushed with fevered, panicky haste through her veins at the thought of being isolated, completely marooned from society, except for the man she had just married. They were to spend their honeymoon in a villa set upon the edge of the lagoon that was used by the Tempera family during the hot summer months. She had been aghast when Leo had suggested it, but her protest, owing to her father's presence, had been mild; her acceptance of the plan all part of the deal to keep Enrico Domini's volatile temper sweet.

In a quiet, subdued mood, she allowed Sara to help her out of the costly wedding finery and into a dress of blue and white checked gingham in which she had the appearance of a troubled infant. Sara was blind to the nuances of expression chasing across her sister's face; she was preoccupied with the wedding dress, fingering the material with admiration and envy.

'How I wish I could wear this dress for my wedding!' she yearned over the rich damask, 'but even if it were allowed I couldn't get into it,' she decided petulantly, 'the waist is far too narrow.'

'You could always forsake pastries for a while,' Jo replied absently.

'I could, couldn't I?' Sara brightened. 'Do you suppose if I did——' she hesitated, then sighed, 'no, I haven't enough willpower to shed the required number of inches in the time allowed. Vincente is most eager to set a date for our wedding—if he had his way it would take place tomorrow.'

'If only it could,' Jo breathed inaudibly, 'I would get my release that very day! How much easier it would be to bear the bondage of marriage if I knew it was to last for only one day!'

Guests crowded on to the *campo* to wave the happy couple goodbye. It was early evening and as Leo nosed the motorboat down the canal Jo huddled in her seat, beset by cold shivers even though sunshine was dancing upon the water, the canal a long silver ribbon with, foaming in their wake, scintillating diamond spray.

Soon they were out in the lagoon, speeding across its width towards the Lido, a vast, glittering beach resort full of hotels, shops, nightclubs, and even a casino. It seemed a strange choice of abode for a man who cherished his solitude, who seemed to incorporate within himself all the qualities of Venice, her supreme conceit, her patronising pride, her high and mighty façade.

But he sped the length of crowded beaches crammed with sun umbrellas, ice cream vans, shrieking children and barking dogs with a haste indicative of distaste and did not slow down until they had reached a quiet stretch of shore enmeshed in weeds and creepers and littered with tree trunks and many-coloured sea-shells. Here, signs of habitation were few, so it came as no surprise when he sidled the boat into a narrow creek so thickly fringed with weeds and long grass they might have been explorers pushing a way through an uncharted river in some dark, unknown continent.

Without comment, he helped Jo out of the boat, then, retaining her hand in his, he hauled her up a narrow path, through a tangle of wistaria and bougainvillea until they emerged into a lawned garden with, set in its middle, a white creeper-covered villa, skilfully placed to gain the maximum ventilation in the heat of summer. The impressive structure was topped by overlapping double roofs, upcurving like sails ready to take the breeze, supported by tall slim pillars that gave to the house an appearance of being delicately balanced, poised between air and sea.

They approached up steps following the rise of the land and entered a cool, black-tiled hall.

'The staircase connects two entrances to the house,' Leo explained, 'one from the front and the other, the one we have just used, from the back. It virtually divides the house into two,' he smiled, seeming to guess that Jo was nervously wondering how many bedrooms it contained. 'Your room is the one under the larger of the roofs,' he supplied. 'The one beneath the smaller roof is mine.'

Relief untied her tongue. 'The wide-spreading roofs are very distinctive,' she stammered, 'like huge wings hovering protectively over a nest.'

He laughed at her description but seemed pleased. 'They were not designed purely for decoration but were logically shaped to collect rainwater for the cistern and to cast welcome shadows during high summer. As there are no internal walls the air circulates. As you can see, the masonry of the walls has been left untouched, again to give added coolness. Heating has not been installed as it was built essentially as a summer house, but water is heated by geyser and fuel for cooking is supplied by gas cylinders. Come, I'll show you to your bedroom and once there I suggest you rest for an hour or two. You look tired, *cara*. It would please me if you were rested enough to enjoy the dinner I have planned especially to celebrate our first night together.'

The bedroom into which he led her was a continuation of the spartan simplicity favoured throughout the villa, holding a modern divan, a couple of chairs and a length of wall consisting entirely of wardrobes with, in its centre, an aperture out of which had been fashioned a dressing-table with mirror, and a glass shelf to accommodate bottles and jars. Underneath was a set of built-in drawers in which to store lingerie.

Leo leant against the door jamb, hands thrust deeply into the pockets of his slacks, and smiled a whimsical smile as he watched her walk across to the window. Patiently he waited for her reaction to the view, then, when she did not speak, he prompted:

'Well, what do you think?'

An indrawn breath was her only reply. Standing splendid in isolation, the villa afforded panoramic views of vivid blue sea and cloudless sky. Below was the green slope leading down to the shell-strewn, wave-kissed, lonely shore that was to be exclusively theirs. It was an ideal love nest, an invincible eyrie, a paradise for lovers—especially for lovers on honeymoon who had need of a beautiful setting, freedom from human distraction, and time to explore the minds of partners who, in spite of having knowledge of each other, might discover their companions possessed of strange, complex facets of nature never previously guessed at.

Leo frowned when he saw her shiver. His voice, terse and clipped, seemed to indicate that there was an edge to his patience.

'I'll leave you to relax. Perhaps later, when you are rested, you will feel more inclined to voice your appreciation—or lack of it!'

When the door slammed behind him she began mechanically to unbutton her dress. He had sounded upset. Disappointed that she had uttered no word of praise for the villa in the sun whose delights he had expected her to appreciate? She was far too tired to appreciate anything and was especially resistant to voicing any admiration lest her husband should take it as a sign of softening, or even of encouragement.

She dragged weary feet across the room and sank down upon the bed. In one respect she agreed with him. She must sleep if she were to prepare her tired spirit, her weary body and numbed mind for the frightening days—and nights—that loomed ahead.

CHAPTER EIGHT

'ARE you awake, *cara*?'

Jo struggled through half-sleep, dreaming that a huge bird of prey with wings outstretched was hovering over her bed. She stared blankly at the shadowy form, fighting rising panic, and her fear did not subside when Leo's face swam into focus, his dark head thrown into sharp relief by a halo of sun, a huge ball of fire slipping slowly past the window.

'You sleep like a child.' His tone was indulgent, almost paternal, but the eyes sliding across the pale creamy slope of shoulder were not. Made suddenly conscious that she was wearing nothing but a flimsy slip, she blushed, a slow embarrassed tide of pink rising in her cheeks. 'Also you blush like a child,' he teased, 'a contrary child who is at one and the same time liberated and prim.'

'I am not prim!' she denied indignantly, jerking upright in order to prove him wrong. She was hard put to it to appear nonchalant when appraised by bold, appreciative eyes. She slid slim legs from the bed and stood up, searching for some protection, however flimsy, for her scantily clad body.

With a grin he reached for a pale peach negligée lying across the foot of the bed. 'Is this what you are looking for?' He quirked a black eyebrow. 'I don't see the necessity, it is still quite warm.'

It was warm, in fact the room felt unbearably hot, yet Jo snatched it from his outstretched hand as if suffering the chills of winter.

'How did it get here, in any case?' she demanded crossly, belting the negligée tightly around her waist. 'And what, now that I have time to think of it, are you doing in my room? You might have had the decency to knock!'

With a feline ease of movement she found disconcerting, he relaxed upon her bed and raked a cool, possessive glance over her fumbling attempts to fasten tiny buttons at her neck. 'Let me help.' His speed of movement was startling, within the space of a gasp he had abandoned his relaxed pose and sprung to her side with effortless, leonine ease. She backed away, confused by his quick change of attitude from lazy docility to stalking predator all in the space of a few short hours. Her hackles rose. It was the piper who was supposed to play while his benefactor chose the tune! She, not he, should be the one in control.

It was not easy to sound authoritative while brown fingers were fumbling at her throat, wresting with tiny buttons. 'Will you please go now, and don't enter my room again without permission!'

He feigned an expression so pained she was infuriated. 'If I am to be forbidden access to your room how am I to carry out my duties? If you wish the services of a *cicisbeo* you must learn to tolerate my presence while I run your bath and help to brush your hair. See,' with a controlled violence that jarred her nerves he slid aside the wardrobe door, revealing a rack of neatly hung dresses, 'already I have unpacked for you! Next I shall run your bath and while you are soaking I'll put the finishing touches to the dinner I prepared while you were asleep. Come now, little *vespa*,' brown fingers abandoned the buttons in order to cup her infuriated face, 'you must admit that I am keeping to my part of the bargain. To ban me from your bedroom would indicate a reluctance on your part to continue on such a basis—I might even be encouraged to think that the ministrations of a husband would be more to your liking!'

He was enjoying a joke at her expense, Jo fumed, not one whit fooled by a subservience made false by a ring of mockery. He was calling her bluff, daring her to opt for one of two equally unacceptable roles —she could choose to have his shadow constantly dogging her footsteps or agree to accept him as a husband, with all the privileges and intimacies such a status implied. She did not hesitate.

'Very well,' she stared cool contempt, 'by all means carry on with your duties. I'd like my bath in five minutes, please.'

If he was disappointed he did not show it by so much as a flicker of an eyelid. Indeed, her decision seemed to please him, judging from the smile flickering around his mouth and the satisfied tone of his answer.

'So be it, *mia bella contessa*!' He lifted her clenched fist to his lips and brushed it with a kiss.

'Stop that!' She snatched away her hand, then was furious with herself for betraying tension.

When he departed, grinning, in the direction of the bathroom, she sagged down on to the bed feeling drained and completely deflated. He was playing with her emotions as a cat plays with a mouse—a well-fed cat, uncertain whether or not he could manage a further tender morsel. And she *was* tender, very tender, very young, very green. Yet she would never allow him to guess the qualms she was experiencing, the water in her veins, the jelly in her knees, the choking lump that rose to her throat, all warnings of his dangerous presence.

She dragged herself upright and was glad she had when a few seconds later he again entered the room.

'I shall lay out your black dress—what there is of it,' he twinkled. 'Wear it, please, I find it very fetching.'

She gritted her teeth. The black dress had been consigned to limbo, she had instructed Maria not to include it in her luggage as she never intended to wear it again. Someone must have countermanded that order—the someone whose golden eyes were alight with devilment as they challenged her across the width of the room. To refuse to meet his challenge would be an admission of defeat.

'Shall do.' Her indifference was well acted. 'But as there will be just the two of us for dinner it hardly seems to matter which dress I wear.'

Nevertheless she took great pains with her appearance, in spite of the profound contempt she felt for the man with whom she was about to dine. Instinct warned her that she would find need of every weapon in her armoury if she were to successfully combat whatever tricks the baffling Conte had up his sleeve. In common with most Italian men he was fond of playing cards. Often Jo had watched and marvelled at his daring while playing bridge, bidding boldly on hands of little strength, bluffing his competitors into losing their confidence, taking his time to plan out his campaign, counting the tricks that were certain to be his, the top trumps, the aces, then cleverly manoeuvring so that tricks were gained that ought never to have been his. His consummate skill was measured by the value he extracted from cards of small significance. Only now was she beginning to realise how cleverly he incorporated the same technique into everyday life; the thrust and parry, the skilled judgment, were arts he had cultivated to a nicety. She would need to keep a sharp lookout for recognised moves and be ready to block each one with the appropriate counter-move.

She went downstairs looking coolly beautiful, but with every nerve vibrant, ready to alert the senses at the first hint of danger. Leo met her in the hall and escorted her into the dining-room. Alarm bells jangled in her mind when she was confronted by an atmosphere reminiscent of a sultan's harem. He guided her towards a beautifully appointed table set with silver cutlery engraved with the Tempera crest—the twin-headed lions with a cold glance that seemed to follow her everywhere. Dark blue candles, displayed with satanic sophistication in sconces of solid silver, flickered with devilish glee across diamond cut crystal goblets, their beauty reflected upon the surface of a table satined with the patina of age. A glorious centrepiece of freshly gathered roses spilled virginal white against cool green foliage—a pungent, forceful reminder of her bridal bouquet. Dim, seductive lighting, romantic background music barely audible to the ear, and a suave, watchful companion, his dark profile strikingly outlined against the whiteness of his dinner jacket, all combined to make an attack upon her senses, resulting in a frantic, panicky warning being transmitted to her brain: *Watch out!*

A deep breath helped steady stampeding nerves into a steady trot, so that his keen eyes gleaned no information from her face as she accepted with languid ease the champagne he poured into her glass. She sipped appreciatively, then dispelled the intimacy surrounding them by observing:

'Isn't it rather dark in here? I like to see what I'm eating—could we please have more light?'

His eyes narrowed, weighing up, she judged, whether the request had been made out of nervousness or necessity. She rejoiced inwardly when, with a small shrug of annoyance, he complied with her wishes by pressing the switch of a small table lamp tucked away in a far corner of the room.

He left her in peace while they enjoyed their meal, which was simple but expertly cooked— prawn cocktail enlivened by a tangy sauce, tender steak accompanied by a crisp salad and a dessert of Kirsch-flavoured raspberries smothered in cream. Jo drank recklessly, then, realising that this was pleasing him, covered the top of her glass with her hand when he made to top it up.

'No more for me, thank you.'

'Don't you like champagne?' he queried, raising one eyebrow in the devilish quirk she had begun to dread.

'Yes, of course, but I've had sufficient, thank you.'

'Nonsense,' he overruled, removing her hand from the glass in order to pour a stream of golden bubbles into the crystal goblet. Rashly, she lifted it to her lips and drained it dry, savouring its effervescence, only to feel nonplussed when he filled up her glass once again. 'I felt sure this wine would be an appropriate choice,' he grinned. 'Champagne has an equal number of followers in heaven and in hell.'

'And to which of those places do you consider I belong?' She tilted her chin, exposing a slender curve of throat he seemed to find captivating. Slowly his eyes caressed a creamy slope of shoulder, then plunged to continue the exploration he had begun the first time she had worn the dress.

'Who knows precisely where angels dwell?' he murmured, his eyes upon the deeply plunging cleavage between her breasts.

To her annoyance her emotions erupted into utter confusion, forcing her to fight to suppress a burning tide of colour rising into pale cheeks. Agitated by his deliberately intimate mood, she reached for her glass, hoping the sudden movement would distract his attention, but her fingers missed the bowl, connected with the stem, and sent the glass crashing on to the table. A stream of golden liquid ran swiftly across the shiny surface and over its edge, straight into Leo's lap.

'*Damnation!*' Instinctively he jumped to his feet to avoid the worst of the spill. Jo grabbed a napkin and ran to help, babbling her apologies while she dabbed surplus liquid from his jacket.

'How clumsy of me! I'm terribly sorry, that was unforgivably careless ...'

A hand clamped down upon each of her shoulders and drew her upright until her troubled eyes were staring into a face no longer mocking, eyes kindling golden flame, a mouth set almost grim.

'Jo! *Io ti amo!*' he groaned, pulling her forward until her head was resting against his heart. Before she could pull away his arms tightened around her waist, she felt the heat of his hands flat against the cool bareness of her back as he bent his head in search of her lips. It was a powerfully virile kiss that drew unwilling response from the very tips of her toes, then proceeded to rage rampant through her helpless body. She was nothing if not human, as susceptible as the next girl to a scene set for seduction —the magic of candlelight, the heady scent of roses, romantic music that aroused yearnings so new to her they were unrecognisable, intoxicating wine that had weakened her defences and left her vulnerable to the advances of her savagely-attractive husband.

Afloat on a cloud of champagne, she stretched on tiptoe to slide her arms around his neck and fired his passion to melting point by returning kiss for kiss, answering need with still more urgent need, heightening the hunger within him with abandoned caresses.

She did not protest when he swept her from her feet to carry her upstairs to her room. Gently, almost reverently, he laid her upon the bed, murmuring hoarse endearments while he unzipped her dress, then, with one quick flick of the wrist, consigned it to a far corner of the room.

The expertise with which this action was carried out reacted like a shock of ice water upon Jo's seduced senses.

'No!' She began to struggle and turned on her side in an attempt to wriggle out of his arms. It was then that she felt the fiery imprint of his lips upon her shoulder as, drawn irresistibly to the devil-dark mole, he murmured:

'How I have longed to do that, *cara*! How does it feel to be branded by the devil?'

'Utterly degrading!' she spat, managing, with the advantage of surprise, to escape his loosened grasp. With her back turned towards him she shivered her way into a negligée, uttering condemnation in a spate of angry words. 'Some of the blame must be mine, I don't understand why I allowed it to happen ... How simple you must think me, a naïve idiot, one whose head is easily turned by flattery, by a stage set for seduction! You played your hand brilliantly, *signore*, masterminded all the tricks, discovered I was vulnerable, then exploited my poor head for wine for all you were worth! But mercifully I recovered my senses in time to trump your tricks!' She swung round, searching for his outline in the darkened room, and found him gazing out of the window into a dark velvet sky. He was silent, tense, uncannily still.

'Please remember in future,' she stormed at his unresponsive back, 'that I am the one who holds all the aces. Papà paid you to marry me and I'm never going to allow you to forget it!'

He strode towards her, his face strained and very weary. She backed away, but was cornered when she came up against solid wall. When Leo reached out to touch her she flinched away and his mouth tightened. However, his grip upon her shoulder was kind.

'Don't say any more just now, Jo, not while you are in a temper. I can understand your feeling shocked, puzzled, a little ashamed, perhaps, but you have no reason to be, child, for are not our passions ourselves? A moment ago you demonstrated that you can be a passionate, generous lover—if ever you allow yourself to be. All you need is more time, while I, on my part, should have shown more patience. Sleep on it, Jo.'

She was afraid she was going to cry, sobs were crowding her throat causing an aching pain which, however much she swallowed, would not be eased. Then anger came to her aid, although what she had intended to be a lighthearted laugh developed into a grating in her throat.

'Really, *signore*, you speak as if you were addressing a child! I'm no stranger to passion, nor am I easily shocked. You are so pitifully old-fashioned in outlook,' she forced a stiff smile. 'Few girls of my age remain virgins in these enlightened days!'

Lightly, his thumbs moved over her shoulders. 'Why are you trembling? Are you cold?' he surprised her by asking.

'No,' she jerked.

'Are you afraid of me?' he continued calmly.

'Of course not!'

'Then why are you trembling?'

She pulled out of his grasp, ran across the room and flung the door open wide. 'If I am trembling, *signore*, it's certainly not with fear. What would you say,' her chin tilted defiantly as he crossed towards her, 'if I were to tell you that, had you succeeded in seducing me, you would not have been the first man to do so?'

He paused a foot away, subjecting her to a steady stare. 'If that is a hypothetical question then an answer would be superfluous—but if it is based upon fact ...'

'Yes,' she goaded, 'what then?'

He reached out to encircle her throat within gentle fingers before menacing in a mildly pleasant manner: 'I should quite probably strangle you.'

CHAPTER NINE

Jo was stretched out on a lounger at the edge of the swimming pool watching Leo cleaving through aquamarine water, his strokes clean and powerful. He had already swum the length of the pool about two dozen times, yet his movements were relaxed and tireless. It seemed quite likely he would continue swimming for ages yet. They had been at the villa for three days and not once during that time had he referred to the incident that had occurred on the first traumatic night. He had reverted to treating her with paternal indulgence, respecting her wish to be alone, making not the slightest demur when, each morning after breakfast, she had disappeared down the path leading to the shore to continue her exploration of the many small coves, to search for unusual sea-shells or just sit for hours dabbling her feet in the lukewarm sea.

But after three days, her explorations exhausted, solitude had begun to pall, so this morning she had surprised him by lingering over breakfast until curiosity had prompted him to ask:

'You seem to be at a loose end, have you nothing planned for today?'

'Er .... not really. I may go down to the beach later.'

'Why not join me for a dip in the pool, then after

lunch we could go for an outing?'

She dithered. The casually extended invitation had held not the slightest hint of urgency, her acceptance or refusal, it seemed, was a matter of complete indifference to him. Consequently, her acceptance was equally casual.

'I might as well, I suppose . . .'

Since the day after their arrival at the villa a maid had come each day from a nearby village. She did not live in, but arrived in time to cook breakfast and left each evening after dinner. She appeared at Jo's side bearing a tray holding a large jug of freshly-made lemonade and a plateful of almond biscuits.

'Thank you, Dina,' Jo smiled her pleasure as she heaved into a sitting position. 'Leave the tray on the table, will you, I'll pour out when the signore joins me.'

Dina returned her smile and bobbed a curtsey, but as she walked away her simple features wore a perplexed frown. The *signore*'s young wife was so beautiful, yet how, she wondered, did the English manage to keep their island populated? For three whole nights the *signore* and his bride had occupied separate bedrooms and for three whole days the *signora* had wandered off on her own, leaving her new husband alone in the villa. Her own husband had refused to believe her when she had told him of their sleeping arrangements. 'No, no,' he had pooh-poohed, 'the Conte is too virile a man to adopt the life of a celibate, especially not on his honeymoon. The strain of it would be too much for him—after all, is it not widely known that such a situation can affect a man's brain?' Still, Dina's frown lightened, at least today they had not gone their separate ways, so perhaps tonight ...!

Leo heaved out of the water and stood teetering on the edge of the pool, flexing his muscles while hot sun dried rivulets of water from skin tanned brown as a nut. Jo averted her eyes from his whipcord body, wondering how she could ever have been misguided enough to liken him to a toothless tomcat. Granted, this lion had no roar, but she knew to her cost that he had teeth, teeth that had bitten gently into her skin to inflict the pain of ecstasy. A flood of colour accompanied the memory and she reached for the jug of lemonade, hoping her blush would go unnoticed. But nothing she did seemed to escape his keen glance.

'You look hot.' He dropped down on to the lounger next to hers. 'Perhaps you should seek more shade,' he frowned, 'your pale skin is not yet acclimatised to our heat.' His solicitude grated upon nerves sparked into expectant life by vibrant kisses and a wildly arousing touch; in three whole days they had not quietened down, her pulses still jerked at his approach, her spine tingled if he so much as brushed her arm with his sleeve, and her wayward heartbeats became annoyingly erratic when occasionally her eyes collided with his golden, enigmatic gaze. She despised her weakness. Irritation was evident in her voice when she enquired:

'How much longer must we remain here?'

His face appeared to darken as cloud drifted across the sun. 'You are bored with the villa already?' he asked lightly. 'Perhaps the fault is mine for neglecting your entertainment. I am a devotee of solitude, but I'm apt to forget that others do not share my preference. As we shall be remaining here for a further two weeks I must remedy the error.'

'Another two weeks!' Jo gasped, her eyes wide with dismay. 'Do we have to? Why can't we return to Venice before then?'

'Because the *palazzo* is in the process of having its foundations strengthened, an exercise which entails the building of a watertight caisson around the building so that concrete may be injected into the foundations.'

Her lips compressed. 'You've wasted no time in making use of my dowry! Were you afraid Papà might change his mind?'

'Not at all,' he assured her smoothly, shrugging aside the insult. 'It is simply that such work can be carried out only at certain times of the year and this happens to be one of those times.'

'It's probably a case of good money being wasted,' she scoffed, impelled for some reason to upset his damnable composure. 'According to experts, Venice is slowly sinking into the lagoon.'

Gravely he nodded. 'There are many places in the city where columns and doorways, once at ground level, are now well below it. Often, when paving stones are removed, the remains of another street built in the Middle Ages when the lagoon was lower are found about a yard below. All over the city one may find evidence of rising water—balconies and windows that have had to be heightened, stone animals with paws awash by the tide, and many damp, rotting brick walls. The sinking process could be arrested, but only at phenomenal expense. At present, we Venetians are more concerned with keeping our city afloat than with rescuing her from drowning.'

It was silly to feel resentful of a city, yet obviously the subject of Venice and her wellbeing was constantly in the forefront of his mind, to the exclusion of all others. Venice, Bride of the Sea, was Leo's true and only bride and he would do anything, make any sacrifice, to ensure the safety of even one small part of it.

She jumped to her feet and stood, rounded and lovely in a curve-hugging bathing suit golden as the sun, and told him abruptly, 'I've had enough of sunbathing, I'm going inside.' Puzzled by her obvious ill humour, Leo nodded agreement, then watched, frowning, as she flounced out of sight.

Moodily, Jo stared around her bedroom wondering why she was feeling so unsettled, so nervy, so unlike her usual confident self. She crossed the room to stare gloomily out of the window, trying to decide what to do. The prospect of going down to the beach loomed uninviting; she had already explored its possibilities to the utmost, and so too, the gardens and the house. So the day yawned dull and depressing. Then she recalled Leo's suggestion that they might go on an outing and her spirits lifted. The suggestion had been casually put—he might even have forgotten—nevertheless she had better be prepared just in case he should come in search of her.

She showered, then spent a few minutes deciding what to wear. He had not indicated in which direction they might go, but hoping he might suggest a visit to the Lido she plumped eventually for a cotton sundress, green to match her eyes, with a short matching jacket in case there should be a breeze. Comfortable white sandals and a pouch bag that could be carried over her wrist were all the accessories needed to complete an outfit that was chic, gay and functional.

She sat down to wait, silently urging Leo to come and fetch her, so that when eventually he did rap upon the door she flew to open it, then waited with suppressed excitement for him to speak.

Slightly taken aback by her swift appearance, he hesitated, then smiled, well pleased. 'Good girl! As you are ready, we can set off immediately.'

'Where are we going?' Eagerly she fell into step. 'And how are we going to get there?'

'By car, of course,' he answered her last question first. 'Didn't I mention that the villa is not far from the main road and that we keep a car garaged here permanently?'

'A car!' she said eagerly. 'In that case, we could go as far as——'

'The Lido?' he quizzed, his lips curling upwards.

'How did you guess I wanted to go there?' she faltered.

'Dear Jo,' he teased, 'you have the look of an infant anticipating a day at the seaside. If you were not so fashionably dressed I might be tempted to supply you with a bucket and spade!'

The run down to the beach resort was both interesting and invigorating. Leo's powerful, long-nosed sports car purred along, eating up miles of empty road and Jo, who lately had begun to wonder how the impoverished Conte could afford the luxury of a summer villa, was prompted to wonder further about the ownership of such a ruinously expensive car. Following this trend of thought, she blurted impulsively:

'Leo, why don't you get a job?'

Ever so slightly he swerved off course. 'I thought I had one,' he answered mildly.

'You are deliberately misunderstanding me,' she retorted. 'I know you consider yourself to be fully employed looking after your family's interests, but when I speak of a job I mean a job that *pays*!'

'Don't all jobs pay in one way or another?' He slanted her an amused look. She fell into puzzled silence. Leo, though reputedly impoverished, nevertheless maintained a high standard of living—a villa, a car, a private gondola, priceless heirlooms housed within the *palazzo*, numerous servants employed to do his bidding, all were proof that he did not go short of cash from somewhere. Yet obviously he had no intention of discussing his financial position. Improvements to the *palazzo* were being paid for by her dowry, but how, she pondered, was he managing to pay for the rest?

But it was not a day to favour moody conjecture. The car was purring the length of a road running alongside an expanse of sea, glass-smooth, sparkling with a brilliance that hurt the eyes as it was caught by the glare of the midday sun. Through gaps in the foliage Jo caught glimpses of beaches crowded with sun-lovers, promenades lined with restaurants protected by gay striped awnings and the towering façades of hotels, brazenly modern, impudently defying the mediaeval majesty of Venice dimly outlined across the water.

He parked the car near the sea-front. 'The day is yours,' he told her, indulgent as a father prepared to reward an obedient child, 'do what you will with it.'

'Let's just stroll,' she begged, captivated by glimpses of streets lined with wistaria and bougainvillea, wishing they could be here at night to see the effect of fairy lights hung in loops and cascades, twinkling with gaudy brilliance against the dark sky. She inhaled a deep breath of shrimp-flavoured, salt-tanged air, her feet pitter-pattering rapidly as she tried to keep up with Leo's rangy stride. He seemed deep in thought as he strode, head down, hands plunged deeply into his pockets, sparing not a glance for the exciting modernity of their surroundings.

'Would you mind slowing down a little?' she gasped, trailing a pace behind him. He stopped so abruptly she cannoned into him and would have stumbled but for his quick grasp upon her elbow.

'How thoughtless of me,' he frowned, very much put out by his unintentional discourtesy. 'I didn't realise——' He broke off, spotting a vacant table in a nearby pavement café. 'Sit here while I order some refreshments—you look hot. Fool that I am for rushing you through this midday heat!' As sun rays fell upon her hair, firing its dark red beauty into glowing life, he shot suddenly, 'Why aren't you wearing a hat?'

'I didn't think a hat would be necessary,' she confessed. 'It felt so cool up in the hills.'

'Let me move your chair closer under the sun umbrella,' he instructed. After she had complied he ordered, 'Now sit there and don't move until I get back.'

By the time he returned Jo had been served lemonade and was savouring its coolness through a straw. When his shadow fell across the table she looked up and saw that he was laughing. A trifle shamefacedly she apologised, 'I ought to have waited for you, but I was parched.' Like a satisfied kitten she sat back and licked a small pink tongue around her lips. 'I asked the waiter to bring you a drink too,' she indicated a second glass, 'you'll enjoy it.'

'No, thank you.' His glance flickered with obvious distaste over the glass full of violently-green liquid. 'Here!' He tossed what looked like a bundle of straw into her lap. 'That was the least conspicuous object I could find, I hope it fits.'

It was a sun-hat fashioned out of plaited straw, high-crowned, its wide brim left abruptly unfinished so that when Jo tried it on a fringe of straw fell across her face, reminding him of an urchin Huckleberry Finn.

'How do I look?' she giggled.

He raised his eyes in despair. 'At one with your surroundings.' His look disparaged everything within his vicinity. The fastidious Conte in his impeccable suit, silken shirt and flowing tie was distinctly out of tune.

With her usual impetuosity, she leant towards him and proffered: 'I've often thought you would benefit by occasionally adopting a less staid attitude in public.'

'Staid . . .?' His nostrils flared.

'Oh, well, dignified, if you prefer—they're one and the same thing really. You don't like it here, do you?'

'I have never professed affinity with sticky buns, gaudy shops, poisonous drinks,' he cast a further disgusted look at the offending lemonade, 'howling children bulging up to the ears with icecream, and their yelling parents supposedly out for a day's enjoyment yet exasperated to the point of murder by their ill-behaved offspring. However,' he sighed, 'for your sake I will try to put up with them, just this once.'

'Why not try to enjoy it, just this once?' she retorted impudently. 'Just for today, couldn't you try to forget that you are Il Conte Tempera and pretend to be a young man of no particular standing intent upon seeking fun. We could pretend we've just met,' she sparkled, carried away on a tide of rash impetuosity, 'two strangers thrown together by accident, with a whole day at their disposal to get to know one another. But you would have to cast off your starched image or it wouldn't work!' she declared with engaging candour. 'To get rid of your jacket and tie might be a good way to start.'

For a few perilous moments she thought she was

about to be slated for her impudence. Expressions of pride warring with temptation crossed his face and as he hesitated something about her animated expression helped him to reach a decision. Showing a hint of self-consciousness she would never have associated with the haughty Conte, he drew off his tie, slipped it into his pocket, then shrugged broad shoulders out of his jacket.

'Satisfied?' he quizzed.

Tapping the tip of her nose with a thoughtful finger, Jo frowned. 'There's something still not quite right,' she puzzled. Then her face brightened. 'Try rolling up your sleeves.'

'Rolling up my ...?'

'*Sleeves*,' she insisted firmly.

With great reluctance he removed silver-crested links from immaculate cuffs and proceeded to roll very expensive blue silk over his forearms. When he had reached past his elbows, she leant across and rather shyly undid the three top buttons of his shirt. The improvement was startling. Bare brown throat rising from out of a winged collar, a tangle of black hairs exposed upon a broad chest, muscles rippling under silk, all combined to make him look relaxed and very much younger. The transformation was complete when he grinned, his white, even teeth outstanding against a tanned skin.

'I feel like a soldier deprived of his uniform, uncertain who I am, and unsure how I am expected to behave. Decently dressed I felt civilised, whereas now ...!' He shrugged, leaving the rest to her imagination.

Jo almost choked on the last of her lemonade. What had she done? Fervently, she wished she could learn to think before she spoke. The courteous Conte she could handle—she was not so sure about this rakish image conjured up at her own foolhardy request!

CHAPTER TEN

As they sauntered along the promenade, Leo took Jo's hand and she did not object. With sun dancing a lively jig upon the water, sky blue as a madonna's cloak, and the sights and sounds of merriment all around them, it was surprisingly easy to forget that the man whose fingers were curled around her own was Il Conte Leonardo Tempera and not one of her casual, undemanding student friends.

Leo seemed to have cast off dignity with his coat, his eyes behind smoky glasses smiling as he looked down at her, not with paternal indulgence, but showing the spontaneous grin an attracted man might bestow upon an attractive girl. Her spirits rose light as her footsteps as she tripped alongside him, pointing out the grace of a seagull outlined in flight against a backcloth of cloudless sky, pausing to worry over a crying infant who seemed to have become detached from his parents, then murmuring her relief when, just as she was urging Leo to intervene, a worried father approached to scoop the distressed child into his arms.

'You have a caring heart, Jo. The welfare of others, even those who are unknown to you, means a great deal, does it not? This is a very unusual trait to be found in a girl such as yourself brought up in what most people would consider the lap of luxury.

Who instilled within you such concern? Not your father. In common with most men of his standing he seems too wrapped up in business affairs to spare much time for introspective thought, while Sara,' he hesitated, wishing to be kind, 'has always seemed to me a little self-centred.'

They were leaning their elbows upon a low wall, looking down upon an anthill of humanity spread across the sands. There was none of the usual distaste reflected in his expression as he watched the antics of families fighting for their pleasure, jealously guarding their conquered strips of territory from encroaching invaders. It was a completely new world to him, Jo realised. An insight into the difficulties experienced by the common herd, the struggle for breathing space never encountered by the man to whom the huge, empty palace of Tempera was home and who, up until now, had considered solitude and space were rights granted to every man. The realisation caused her a pang of pity—the very last emotion she would normally have associated with the imperious Conte.

'My mother took great pains to impress upon me the need for compassion towards others less fortunate than ourselves,' she explained haltingly. 'If that sounds patronising it isn't meant to be,' she rushed on, 'my mother was of a nature so loving and giving she would have reacted the same even if we'd been living in poverty. Money, possessions, status, were of secondary importance to her. I remember asking once, with all the anxiety of childhood: "Mammà, what will become of Papà if ever he should lose his money?" Her answer chased from my mind every childish fear. "Riches have wings, my darling," she replied, "sometimes they fly away. But children are poor men's riches, so long as he has the love of his children he will never know poverty."'

She lapsed into silence and Leo's grip upon her fingers tightened. 'How old were you when she died?' he asked.

'Twelve,' she sighed. 'The worst possible age.' Then, unwilling to linger on a subject still tender, she questioned, 'And what about you? I've never heard you speak of your mother. Do you, too, find such memories painful?'

She was startled by his careless shrug. 'I have no memories,' he surprised her. 'My mother died when I was born.'

'Oh . . . I'm sorry.'

He smiled, teeth flashing white against nut-brown skin. 'Tender heart,' he teased. 'Why should you be sorry? What is that saying you English have: What one has never had one cannot miss?'

'But that simply isn't true!' she objected, touched to the heart by a picture she had conjured of a baby nursed in strange arms; the cuts and bumps of an exploring toddler left unhealed by a mother's kiss; the worries of a schoolboy having no one in which to confide; the stresses of adolescence and the struggle into maturity—all situations in which a mother's understanding were priceless. 'Perhaps your father tried twice as hard, as mine did, to make up for your loss?'

He shook his head, allowing more loneliness than

he knew to colour his tone as slowly he explained, 'I saw very little of my father, he spent most of his time abroad, leaving me in the charge of nurses, and tutors—and my aunt, of course. According to her, my father resented me, could never forgive me for taking my mother's life in exchange for my own. If he had stayed in Venice, if we had been given the opportunity to get to know one another, perhaps I could have replaced her in some small way, but it was not to be.'

'Your aunt told you *that*!' Jo choked, horrified by the insensitive treatment meted out to a motherless boy. No wonder the lonely child had grown into an even more solitary man. Guilt had been heaped upon his shoulders. Time and tradition had graced him with a veneer of self-confidence, yet with such a history he must surely carry inside of him a feeling of guilt, a conviction even, that he had no right to happiness. Compassion brimmed over. Impulsive as ever, she advised him fiercely:

'I don't know how you can bear to continue living in a house full of such unhappy memories! Why don't you close it up, forget that it ever existed or, if that isn't possible, make up for your lonely childhood by filling the *palazzo* with children so that their happy laughter, their stampeding footsteps, will chase out all your childhood ghosts!'

He threw his head back and laughed so loudly everyone in their vicinity smiled and looked ready to join in. Startled, Jo looked up, then caught her breath. Etched against a background of blue sky his profile rejected dark, attractive appeal. Muscles rippled in his throat and as he continued to laugh his chest heaved, dislodging from a tangle of dark hairs a silver medallion that swung crazily on a fine silver chain.

'Oh, darling Jo!' he grinned, bending down to peer into her indignant face. 'I would like that! I really would . . .'

Suddenly, as they stared into each other's eyes, everything seemed to hush, waves lapped silently upon the shore, children's screams faded to a whisper, their parents' shouts mere echoes of what they had previously been. Even the birds' raucous cries seemed muted, the chimes of an ice cream vendor advertising his wares deadened by a thudding noise, a heavy pounding filling Jo's ears. When he removed his sunglasses, then disposed of hers, she found she was staring into eyes no longer alight with laughter but intensely dark, mirroring fathomless feeling.

'A home full of happy children,' he spelled out slowly. 'If only it were possible, Jo. It could be,' he insisted softly, 'if you could only bring yourself to accept me as a husband.'

At that moment she recognised the pounding in her ears as the beating of her heart. She bit her lip, hovering between mistrust of his silvered tongue and an urgent will to believe. He sounded at that moment as if he were prepared to forsake even Venice, his bride of the sea, if in exchange he could have his very mundane wish. She shook off his spell. What he was experiencing was mere whimsical longing, a momentary urge that would pass, leaving embarrassment in its wake if she were fool enough to take him seriously. Sincerity was as much a stranger as was laughter to the inhabitants of the Palazzo Tempera.

So she broke from his compelling glance, uttered a shaky laugh, and completely shattered the spell by declaring brightly, 'I'm hungry, aren't you? Let's find something to eat.'

Leo's only physical reaction was a slight tightening of his grip before he set her free, then, in a tone so matter-of-fact she blinked, he agreed with her suggestion.

'Very well, we'll try one of the hotels along the front.'

'Oh, but ...' She dug in her heels, resisting the pressure he was exerting upon her elbow as he attempted to guide her away from the promenade.

'But what?' he quizzed, replacing her sunglasses as she frowned against the glare.

'Couldn't we have a picnic?'

His doubtful look confirmed her suspicion that he had never known the childish pleasure of an alfresco meal, with a salt-tanged breeze adding flavour and lack of ceremony bestowing piquant freshness to plain fare.

'If that is really what you want,' he conceded reluctantly.

'Oh, it is, it is!' She tugged his arm in her eagerness. 'There are shops down the side streets where we can buy bread and cheese—and pickles, if you like pickles?'

'I do.' He sounded surprised by his own admission.

'And a poke of shrimps would be nice,' she cajoled, sensing his weakening, 'and some fruit to finish off.'

Not only did they find all that they required, they also bought swimwear and two large bath-towels before making their way back to the beach. But after ten minutes of stepping over browning bodies in a fruitless search for space, Leo rebelled.

'Let's go back to the car—I know of a private beach nearby where we can relax and be undisturbed. The owner, a friend of mine, is away at present, but if he were here I know that permission to trespass would be gladly given.'

Jo relented with a nod. He had behaved beautifully considering his dislike of crowds and his abhorrence of modern-day noise. The least she could do was to fall in with this one solitary suggestion when, during the whole of their time here, he had set out expressly to please her.

The cove was a mere ten minutes' drive away, but they might have stepped into another world when they parked the car and began descending a sloping path leading down to a crescent of fine sand bearing not one human imprint upon its smooth surface. They stacked their basket of goodies beneath cool foliage, then went behind rocks to discard clothing that had begun to feel cumbersome in the heat.

Jo emerged feeling slightly selfconscious in a one-piece bathing suit patterned with garish, fullblown roses, its mixture of colours having been the least offensive she could find among garments piled high upon the counter of a one-roomed shop. Doubtfully, she looked down. At the time it had seemed an unnecessary extravagance to seek out a more expensive suit—after all, her drawers at the villa held at least a dozen swimsuits and this cheap one had been purchased for only one unforeseen swim. Yet, with one huge rose enclosing her waist within the grip of hideous lime green petals, she began having second thoughts.

Her feet felt weighted as slowly she began walking down to the beach, dreading the sight of Leo's eyebrows elevating and his lips quirking as he tried to contain amusement. But when she looked up and saw him sidling from behind a rock it was she who had to laugh at the tall, usually elegant figure wearing an expression of utter disgust as he peered down at shorts made up of striped material in violently clashing colours offensive to the eye. His expression was just too much. Laughter began as a choked gurgle deep within her throat, then spluttered past compressed lips to emerge as an hilarious shout that might have disturbed the slumberers on the Lido beaches.

He was not amused. Showing a glint in his eye that boded ill for Jo, he stepped forward and accused, 'I ought to have known better than to allow you to shop for me! You chose this diabolical garment deliberately, did you not?'

'I'm afraid so,' she spluttered, holding her sides as a fresh spasm of laughter rendered her helpless.

'Mine,' she gasped, indicating her own costume, 'was the best of a bad bunch, so I searched out something equally hideous for you in case you should be tempted to make comparisons!'

Instinct warned her to run even before he made his first step towards retaliation. She flew down the beach with a speed that kept her within inches of his outstretched hands and plunged into the water to dive swiftly as a minnow determined to outwit a shark. But gradually his dark shadow overtook her and she was enmeshed by hands that gripped her waist, then showed no mercy as they administered a ducking that left her breathless. Desperately she clutched rock-hard shoulders and pleaded in small breathless gasps:

'Please, Leo, no more! I'm sorry, truly I am, she half laughed, half choked, 'so no more ducking, *please!*'

'You *are* a bitch.' Never had the words been spoken with such a tender intonation.

She went very still within the circle of arms that tightened fractionally before surrendering her to the emotionless embrace of the sea. Minutes later all she could see of him was his dark head bobbing above the waves as he directed all his energies and frustrations towards a battle with the waves.

She was dry and stretched out on her towel by the time he returned. He dropped down on to the towel she had draped upon the sand a careful yard away, then, catching her peeping through lowered lashes, he requested politely, 'I'm hungry, do you mind if we eat now?'

Experiencing a mixture of relief and disappointment, she scrambled to her feet and ran to fetch the basket, avoiding his eyes as she shared out the bread and cheese, shrimps and fruit while he uncorked a bottle of wine. Two plastic cups were utilised as goblets for wine that flowed like soothing nectar down parched throats. Handsful of crusty bread were torn from a long, cigar-shaped loaf, delectable hunks of cheese delivered a sharp bite upon the tongue, delicious shrimps were denuded of their armour, then slowly savoured before teeth sank into peaches so luscious the juice overflowed on to their chins. Surreptitiously, Jo wiped hers away with sand-encrusted fingers, then, replete and contended, they both rolled on their backs to laze, enclosed within an atmosphere of silent companionship, a feeling of togetherness too ethereal, as yet, to be named. They slept like weary children with arms outstretched, their fingertips almost, but not quite, bridging the yard of dividing sand.

After ten blissful minutes Jo wakened from her nap. Cautiously she moved, bewildered by a trapped sensation, then went very still when Leo stirred in his sleep and tightened his grip around her wrist. She chanced a quick look, wondering if he were feigning sleep, and was disarmed by a small smile of contentment hovering around his relaxed mouth. He looked so defenceless in sleep; it was easy to discover traces of the boy he had once been in thick lashes lying in dark crescents upon high cheekbones. How often those lashes must have swept down to hide tears he had been taught were unseemly in a future Conte. How often his mouth must have quivered with hurt inflicted by his insensitive aunt. And how often his lean frame must have tensed to suppress an urge to run to the father who had rejected him, seeking comfort and a little of the love he had been denied.

Her heart lurched. Leo seemed destined never to enjoy a loving relationship. Even his wife, she recalled bitterly, had been chosen with finance rather than emotion in mind.

She stared down at him, allowing herself the momentary weakness of wondering what it would be like to be loved by such a man. She knew his touch could arouse her to barely endurable heights of passion, the scarring imprint of his kisses would remain on her lips for ever. She shivered, remembering how her body had responded to caresses so expert they had repelled and she had to force her mind to accept the fact that although Leo had made it plain he would not be averse to claiming his rights as a husband, his main objective in marrying her had been the price she carried on her head.

She quivered a sigh, trying to lash up scorn, to arm herself with the hatred she assuredly felt for this man. But the venom seemed to have been drawn from her sting, in place of an armour of hatred she had been left clutching a veil of vulnerability so lacking in protection it could be pierced by the quirk of an eyebrow or a casually flung smile.

She was jerked back to reality by a fixed stare. Embarrassed colour flooded her cheeks. It was stupid to feel panic-stricken, wondering how long he had been awake—there was no possible way he could have read her thoughts!

His words, however, seemed to disprove this theory. Slowly, concentrating his interest upon her heightened colour, he mused aloud, 'Today, in some subtle way, you seem different. Your attitude is gentler, less reserved. Your words are spontaneous expressions of happiness instead of barbs directed by a suspicious mind. You are always beautiful, Jo, but today your face has acquired a special glow.' Though his words were slow his movement was swift as he rolled on his side to throw an arm around her, pinning her to the sand. Mesmerised, her brave resolutions evaporating swift as droplets beneath the sun, she quivered beneath his shadow, straining to cull the will to resist from a weak, traitorous body.

'Today has been wonderful, has it not, *amore mia*?' The magnetism he was projecting was over-powering. Panic clutched at her throat and squeezed it tight. She felt nerveless and weak as an infant utterly dependent upon the whims of its minder. Finding words impossible, she pleaded with her eyes, mutely appealing to him to be kind. She was at that moment blissfully prepared to be taken, to be loved, to be mastered ...!

For long breathless seconds they stared into each other's eyes, conscious of an aura of inevitability, a strong, vital attraction that drew them closer yet at the same time bade them pause to savour for a while joyful anticipation. As his head descended her lashes lowered, shy in case the trail of heat blazing through her body might be reflected in her eyes. His shadow blotted out the sun and she was glad to use darkness as a cloak during the long-drawn-out, almost unendurable seconds of waiting.

Her mouth was quivering, anticipating his kiss, when he uttered a sharp, savage curse and flung away. With his shadow removed the sun blazed down. Jo flinched from its scourge and rolled on her side, fighting an urge to cry as an agony of humiliation ran sword-sharp through her body.

'Come, it is time for us to go.' His touch was impersonal as he helped her to her feet, but she turned her face away, conscious that she was not yet sufficiently in control to hide the ravages of rejection.

She hated the steadiness of his voice, the cool impersonality that contrasted so violently with her own emotions, when casually he suggested, 'Let us return to the villa now. I see no reason why such a pleasant day should not be prolonged, so I have decided that tonight we will return and visit the casino. Would you like that . . .?'

There it was again—the damnable paternal intonation she so resented! Bolstered by temper, she rounded on him. 'As a special treat for an unworldly infant?' she taunted sarcastically, 'or as an apology for insincerity?' She wanted to hurt him, enjoyed the white pinched look around his mouth, the sombre darkness of his eyes. 'By all means let us enjoy what the Lido has to offer.' She tried to make her voice sound eager, as if the prospect he had presented filled her with delight rather than the dread she was actually feeling. If today had been a pattern for days to come she knew she would not stay the pace. Like a jaded Casanova, he had experimented with her emotions, then, showing a humiliating lack of enthusiasm, had decided that she did not measure up to the ghost from his past: Francesca. His rejection was even harder to bear than his persistence had been. But all of life was a lesson and if nothing else this episode had taught her one important lesson—never again to believe him capable of sincerity!

As she followed him towards the car she could not help but wonder why, with a carpet of warm sand beneath her feet, a ceiling of blue sky, and the hot breath of summer on her back, she should be feeling as if it were three o'clock on the morning of a cold, dank, miserable winter's day.

CHAPTER ELEVEN

DINA was displeased with her employer. All during dinner he had picked morosely at his food, sparing barely a glance for his young wife sitting opposite. She had nurtured great hopes that today would bring about a change of attitude between the two and when after lunch they had set off on their outing in such high spirits she had felt certain that the cloud had lifted and that at last the honeymoon was about to begin.

At a nod from the *signore* she whipped a plate from beneath his nose and enquired stiffly, 'Shall I serve dessert now, *signore*?'

'I beg your pardon ...? Oh, none for me, thank you, Dina.' Then, as if suddenly reminded that he was not alone, he added, 'What about you, Jo, are you ready to sample yet another of Dina's delicious concoctions?'

Dina bridled, not one whit mollified as she glanced at the Contessa's pale, unhappy face. She was wearing a dream of a dress, a floating chiffon affair coloured cool leaf green, and from the transparent cape hugging unblemished shoulders her neck rose slender as a stem, her burnished hair, bathed by the rays from an overhead lamp, fiery as her courageous spirit. But her green eyes were sad and the usually tempestuous mouth had quivered noticeably several times during the silent meal. In the space of a few days the Contessa had entered from childhood into womanhood, from a tight bud into a blossom just waiting to be plucked. But the Conte seemed not to have noticed. Was he blind? Or was it that he simply did not want to see?

'Sorry,' Jo smiled her apologies to the anxiously hovering maid. 'I'm sure the sweet you have prepared is excellent, Dina, but I couldn't eat another bite.'

Even the fact that his wife's healthy young appetite had deserted her did not seem to disturb him. With a lack of concern that made Dina fume, he rose to his feet and suggested politely, 'Then as we are both satisfied, we might as well go.'

'*Satisfied!*' Dina murmured under her breath as she stood in the open doorway watching the Conte helping his wife into the car. 'The satisfied do not love, they nod off with boredom!' Her brow wrinkled. And yet boredom had no place in a relationship such as theirs. The tension between them could almost be felt, it was as if they were both foolishly skimming over an ocean whose depths were about to be ravaged by subterranean upheaval!

Earlier in the day Jo had wished she could see the coloured lights strewn across the dark evening sky. But the sight, spectacular though it was, gave her spirits no lift. Since their return to the villa she had fallen into a state of numbed hurt, a quiet, introspective mood Sara would have termed a sulk but which was actually a cloak to protect nerves too raw to bear the pain of probing. Many times she had shied from searching for answers to the questions hammering against the doorway of her mind. Questions such as: Why am I feeling so hurt? Why should the fact that he finds me unattractive matter so much? What possible difference can it make when, at the earliest opportunity, I shall be leaving him?

Once, Jo recalled a childhood memory, she had fought with a cousin who had picked up one of her favourite toys. The girl's mother, much to her own mother's indignation, had remarked coldly: 'Jo, I'm afraid, is a little spoiled, covetous of that which is denied her.'

Had her aunt's assessment been correct? When Leo had tried to put their relationship on a more intimate footing she had spurned him. Was she now coveting the toy she could not have, did she want his attention only because she, in turn, had been spurned?

When Leo drove straight past the casino she turned her head, watching the huge palace of fun receding into the distance. 'It is a little early yet,' he replied to her unspoken question. 'Although the gaming rooms are open the atmosphere will be not quite right. There is a night club not far from here that puts on a passably good cabaret, we will spend an hour or two there, and then make our way to the casino later. Agreed ...?'

He spared her a quick second to turn his attention from the road in order to smile down at her. Her heart jolted, then began beating at a furious rate. 'Very well,' she stammered, 'anything you decide is fine by me.' She then subsided into silence, waging inward war against emotions completely out of control.

Enrico Domini liked his daughters to move in sophisticated circles, consequently Jo was no stranger to affluence. Yet the nightclub into which Leo led her was unlike any she had previously visited, seeming more of an exclusive club, a rich oasis secreted within a strip of bawdy desert and reserved exclusively for the privileged few. While a doorman spirited away the car they were welcomed inside by a beaming manager who immediately summoned a waiter to escort them to a table made intimate by a screen of palm leaves, yet situated conveniently near to the circular dance floor. Lighting was discreet, sufficient glow to enable faces to be recognised if one should wish to recognise, yet dim enough to make deliberate oversight excusable. Thick carpets muffled the footsteps of waiters rushing to pander to the appetites of late diners and Jo's seat, when she sank into it, hugged her within an embrace so comfortable she felt immediately relaxed.

'Champagne...? Leon suggested as the wine waiter hovered.

'Lovely,' she accepted, leaning back in her seat and wriggling her toes, prepared to enjoy the music the small band of musicians was about to play.

The sound that eventually issued was completely attuned to their surroundings, discreetly intimate with a throbbing, romantic beat.

'Would you like to dance?' Leo's offer came as a sweet surprise and was eagerly accepted.

'Yes, please, I'd love to!'

As she slipped into his arms her grandmother's advice came, unsolicited, into her mind. *'Be as honest with yourself as you are with others, Jo!'* It was hard to admit even to herself that all she wanted was to feel his arms around her, to be able to slide her hands across his broad shoulders, to rest her head against his heart and drink in the hard, warm strength of him. At first he remained aloof from her attractions, but as the dance progressed and the floor became crowded he was forced to tighten his protective arm and gradually she felt muscles knotted tensely beneath her outspread fingers beginning to relax as he was wooed by the pleasure of sweet music, an enjoyable atmosphere, and the encouragingly approachable attitude of the girl in his arms.

'Precocious minx ...' His breath tickled her ear. 'Why have you suddenly decided to flaunt your femininity, to parade your very considerable charms before a susceptible husband? I warn you, Jo, that you are acting unwisely. Unless——' He broke off, leaving a question hanging in the air.

Her head began to spin. More than anything in the world she wanted to test his reaction to the tremendous, amazing, even frightening secret she was only now daring to recognise. All day knowledge had been banging on the door of her mind demanding admission, but she had refused it entry. Now, feeling a great sense of relief, she faced the truth behind messages that had been transmitted for days by a pounding heart, racing pulses, vibrant nerves and an agonised yearning which had been nameless. She knew now that its name was love. A glorious, exciting, ecstatic feeling, so strong it had overridden pride and doubt and even the humiliation she had experienced that afternoon.

'Well, Jo?' His lips descended lightly against a pulse throbbing madly at her temple. Riotous emotions erupted and she began to tremble. Within the swaying crowd of dancers their seclusion was such that she was able to press flushed cheeks against his chest and to stammer:

'Leo, something tremendous has happened. I must tell you ... you must know ...'

His perception was such he sensed immediately that some momentous decision had been reached. He pulled her closer and urged, 'I must know what, *cara? Tell me!*'

At that precise moment the music reached its finale with a long-drawn-out crescendo of sound that penetrated their absorption, jogging them into the realisation that they were the last couple remaining upon the dance floor. Reluctantly they drew apart, but he kept tight hold of her hand as he led her back to the table where a green foiled bottle was plunged up to its neck in a bucket of crushed ice. Not once, as they waited until a waiter had decorked the bottle, did his eyes leave her face—a face made even lovelier by a soft glow lighting her eyes, the tremulous lift of her mouth, the rise and fall of colour in her cheeks.

After interminable seconds the waiter finally departed, leaving them alone with two glasses of wine sparkling between them, golden, effervescent, with minute bubbles rising from the depths to explode on to the surface—a wine reserved especially for toasts, for well-wishing, for glorious, exciting occasions. The glint in Leo's eyes told her that he had almost reached the end of his patience. She drew in a deep breath.

'Leo, I——'

'*Leo! Tesoro mio!* I could hardly believe my eyes when I saw you leaving the dance floor! Is it really you?' The voice, shrill, feminine and extremely penetrating, sliced stiletto-sharp between them, demanding a response Leo seemed loath to provide. With a muttered imprecation audible only to Jo, he rose to his feet to extend a polite greeting towards the unwelcome intruder.

'*Buona sera*, Francesca, I hope you are well?'

'*Benissima, caro*, but you could have found that out sooner had you taken the trouble to call. Where on earth have you been these past weeks?'

So this was Francesca!

Jo's senses were alerted by the proprietorial tone in which the question had been voiced. It had not been a light enquiry, more a demand for explanation of absence.

Blandly ignoring what amounted almost to rudeness, Leo nodded to Francesca's escort before replying with polished smoothness.

'Perhaps an introduction will serve as an explanation. Jo,' he smiled down at her bewildered face, 'I would like to introduce two very old friends of mine —Signorina Francesca Pellegrino and her brother, Mario.'

Francesca barely acknowledged Jo, but her brother looked intensely interested, his dark eyes admiring from a distance. His mouth dropped agape, however, when Leo continued, 'Francesca, Mario, allow me to present the Contessa Josephine Tempera—my wife.'

Francesca was extremely attractive, Jo thought, a dark-eyed, black-haired Latin beauty with a full passionate mouth and carefully controlled hour-glass figure. She projected the arrogance of one who took admiration for granted and the poise that only breeding can bestow. She must also be very wealthy, Jo concluded, eyeing a dress that was the product of one of the leading fashion houses, and diamonds flashing at throat, ears and wrists that looked fabulously expensive, if a little ostentatious for an occasion such as this. But Francesca had need of all the poise she could muster in order to weather the blow Leo had dealt. For one stunned moment her eyes flashed over Jo with such resentment in their depths that she shivered, then her blazing eyes settled upon Leo's face, searching his bland expression for signs of humour.

'You are a great joker, Leo,' she husked. 'It *is* a joke, is it not . . .?'

Mario, sufficiently like his sister to have been her twin, shuffled his feet and gave an embarrassed cough. 'May we all sit down?' he suggested awkwardly. 'We seem to be attracting a great deal of attention.'

Jo glanced around and saw that he was right. Every eye was upon them. Leo and Francesca were obviously well known to the club's clientele and the drama of the moment was such that even the discreet Italians had forgotten themselves far enough to gape. During the few moments it took for waiters to fetch extra chairs, Francesca was able to rein in her emotions to the extent of composing her features —but not her eyes. Jo felt their stab upon her face and body as slowly she was examined, assessed, then dismissed as a nonentity.

Francesca's very first sentence was evidence that she intended mischief. Fixing a hard, angry stare upon Leo, she grated, 'As you have made no denial I must assume that you were speaking the truth. But why all the secrecy, *caro*? Did we not agree, during our long and happy association, that there was to be no commitment on either side? Surely,' her voice softened to a silky meaningful purr, 'such old friends as we were entitled to an invitation to your wedding? Or were you perhaps afraid that I might have made a fuss, might have tried to persuade you to change your mind? Knowing how persuasive I can be, Leo, were you afraid that I might do just that ...?'

Jo's heart descended like a stone. In just a few succinct sentences Francesca had painted a portrait of unmistakable intimacy. She had not been naïve enough to imagine Leo a complete celibate, no attractive man could reach his age without having had at least one serious affair. But he might have had the decency to rid himself of surplus female entanglements before taking a wife!

Mario's appalled gasp was partially drowned by the sound of music as the band resumed playing, but Leo's concise reply was not. With a nonchalance Jo found incredible, he leant across to pat Francesca's hand while in a half reproving, half bantering tone, he chided,

'Come now, Francesca, enough of the dramatics! Mario and I are well aware of your penchant for making a great deal of fuss about nothing, but my young wife is not. See how you have shocked her.' His tone was dry as he flicked a glance across Jo's ashen face. 'Child that she is, she has placed the worst possible meaning upon your innuendoes. As for the wedding invitation, you would certainly have received one had you not been visiting Paris at the time the ceremony took place.'

Francesca shrugged off his explanation, seemingly satisfied, now that barbs had been shot, to smile apologies all round, then settle back in her chair with feline grace. 'I will forgive you this time, Leo, *caro*,' she purred, 'but I shall expect prior warning of any future happenings.'

'Such as a marital rift!' Jo muttered beneath her breath, struggling to retrieve remnants of shattered dignity. What a gullible idiot she had been! She ought to feel grateful to Francesca for preventing her from committing the ultimate act of idiocy. Knowing the motive behind Leo's insistence that they should marry, having, as early as this afternoon, been presented with proof of his lingering devotion to Francesca, had she actually been ready to admit to Leo that she had *fallen in love with him*?

Her gratitude towards Mario knew no bounds when politely he asked if she would care to dance. 'Yes, please,' she accepted with alacrity, and swept from the table with chin held high in defiance of Leo's enquiring stare.

Mario was an excellent dancer and though, in her upset state, Jo stumbled once or twice, his expert guidance covered up her mistakes until she was composed enough to concentrate all her mind upon following his lead. She was relieved that, at first, he did not attempt to make conversation but gave her time to adjust, so that when he did finally speak she was able to give him her complete attention.

'My sister and I have been friendly with Leo since childhood. Our two families have always been close, our fathers and grandfathers were business partners, consequently our families visited each other regularly. Which is why Francesca and I are apt to look upon the Palazzo Tempera as a second home—and everything and everyone in it as being of special interest to us.'

'Please don't attempt to vindicate Leo,' she requested gently, 'there is really no need.'

'There isn't?' He looked surprised.

She shook her head. 'None whatsoever,' she confirmed hardly, deciding she owed Leo no loyalty. 'Our marriage was an act of convenience on both sides. It's a long story and I won't bore you with it, but rest assured, *signore*, your sister's innuendoes caused me no grief. Indeed, I found her remarks less than interesting.'

He expelled a soundless whistle. There was something wrong somewhere, he sensed, but as yet he could not guess exactly what it was. But Leo's wife was certainly a product of her race; it would be interesting to discover if she were ice all through or merely frozen on the surface.

As the band swung into a foot-tapping Spanish number he decided to gauge his companion's depth of fun. Whisking her into the centre of the floor, he began stomping out the rhythm with his feet while at the same time twirling, spinning and weaving Jo at arm's length in the manner of a matador brandishing his cloak. Surprise was her first reaction, then elation took over as she entered into the spirit of the dance with all the fervour her supple young body could demonstrate. Excitement rose to fever pitch as she lost herself in the dance, aware yet uncaring that the rest of the dancers had formed a watching circle around the perimeter of the dance floor and were clapping wild encouragement to the spectacular couple, extracting every ounce of enjoyment from their performance. The band repeated the tune once, twice, three times more before, their energies spent, Jo and Mario gasped a laughing protest, whereupon the band responded by sliding into a slow, seductive tune.

As Jo made to leave the floor Mario detained her with a grasp upon her elbow. Pulling her back into his arms, he dared wickedly, 'You have implied that Leo's feelings are a matter of complete indifference to you, but I think he has asked to be punished a little and knowing how possessive an animal he can be, I think I know just the way to do it! Let's flirt a little,' he dared her. 'Leo will be furious, but we might find it enjoyable.'

Temptation was strong and she was as weak as Eve. 'All right, let's!' she agreed recklessly, thereby proving to Mario that she had lied. If she did not care about her husband's opinion she would hardly go out of her way to vex him, he reasoned. She was trying to fool even herself by professing indifference, yet the very lie was proof of Leo's superiority. Mario suppressed a secret smile, he felt no great affection for his sister, but he valued Leo's friendship highly—a friendship he was about to put at risk!

Momentarily shrugging off his misgivings, he pulled her closer and as she snuggled up to him, entering into the spirit of the game, he rested his cheek upon her bright head, reminding himself firmly, as her perfume drifted beneath his nostrils, that the beautiful girl in his arms was the property of his tight-lipped friend whose chilling eyes were following their every movement as they swayed together in time to the music.

It was Jo's idea that Mario and Francesca should accompany them to the casino. Francesca was delighted.

'How kind of you to invite us! Naturally we would love to come.'

Mario's reply was less effusive but equally sin-

cere. Their flirtation was coming along nicely—
with the help of the champagne he was pressing
upon Jo at every opportunity. The one disappointing factor was Leo's change of attitude; instead of
the jealousy Mario had earlier noticed he had, after
an initial coldness, reverted to sitting back and being entertained by Francesca, who was an expert
handler of men. Jo had been quick to sense his lack
of interest, hence her increasing bravado. She knew
she was behaving badly, flirting openly, drinking
too much champagne, but so long as her desperate
unhappiness remained hidden she did not care.

During one rare moment when she and Leo were
left alone he reached for her hand. Carefully examining each perfect fingernail, he observed mildly,
'You are running dangerously close to making a
spectacle of yourself, *cara*. I can understand your
preference for Mario's company, he is a very enter-
taining young man, but do you have to make your
pleasure quite so obvious?'

She turned upon him a look of wide-eyed inno-
cence. 'Surely I'm doing you a favour by keeping
him occupied? You obviously have much to discuss
with his sister.'

'On the contrary,' he objected sharply, 'we are
merely chatting, covering old ground.'

'But that's even better, isn't it?' she countered
sweetly, choking back her hurt. 'How fortunate you
are to have a friend who knows you so well that
conversation is superfluous—so much can be ex-
pressed in long intimate silences!'

CHAPTER TWELVE

THE casino was brash, exciting and so crowded it was easy for Jo and Mario to become deliberately lost. He supplied her with a pile of chips, then proceeded from table to table, explaining the intricacies of each particular game. She had no need to pretend absorption, gambling was new to her, a thrilling fascination that grew as fast as the pile of chips on the table in front of her.

'Beginner's luck!' Mario termed it, as time and time again her chosen number was called and winning chips pushed her way. Intoxicated with success, she was reluctant to leave, but finally yielded to Mario's persuasions when, with a quick glance at his watch, he reminded her, 'It is two o'clock, Jo, I think we'd better start looking for the others, don't you?'

'Perhaps you're right,' she sighed. 'Will you cash these chips for me while I fetch my wrap? I'll meet you in the foyer in about five minutes.'

Mario was a long time returning. A little lost without his support, Jo wandered into the foyer feeling conspicuous without an escort. Noticing a screen of palms, she made towards it, hoping to hide from the curious eyes of people grouped around the foyer chatting idly as they prepared to leave. The hum of voices was all around her, yet as she sought the protection of huge, outspread leaves one voice reached her above the rest, its pitch penetrating even though its tone was subdued. Realising that Francesca and Leo were seated behind the spread of greenery, she jerked away, but her feet remained rooted to the spot as, holding her breath, she waited for Leo's answer to the question she had just heard Francesca put to him.

'Why did you marry her, Leo? She is not of our nationality, not of our culture—indeed, everything about her is directly opposite to the sort of woman with whom you are accustomed to associating.'

'Perhaps that is why.' His light tone gave nothing away.

'Oh, come, Leo, don't be evasive,' Francesca's voice dropped to a husky whisper. 'Am I not entitled to know? For years you have skirted around the subject of marriage and have avoided—with admirable gallantry, I must admit—the wiles of women eager to become the next Contessa. And there have been many, elegant, sophisticated and very worldly, yet along comes this simple English girl who, so far as I can see, has nothing more to commend her than moderate good looks and a somewhat naïve manner, yet you immediately marry her!'

For the life of her, Jo could not have moved away.

'You are a woman of the world, Francesca,' she heard Leo drawl. 'I married Jo for one very obvious reason, surely I have no need to spell out to *you* what that reason is?'

Jo could have screamed her impatience during the long suspended silence that followed. She had begun to suspect that they had moved away and was about to dare a peep around the leaves when a voice so dejected it was barely recognisable as Francesca's replied, 'How I envy you, *mio caro*, and how I wish I could be lucky enough to share the same good fortune! Soon I, too, shall have to marry. Mario and I are an extravagant pair. And why not,' she sounded irritable, 'when we were brought up from birth to believe that money was plentiful? From childhood to adolescence we lived the sort of life expected of the children of a family of high position. It was not until our father died that we learned that there was very little money left and that the only way we could continue with the life-style to which we had become accustomed was to capitalise on our assets, such as they are.'

She gave a hard laugh. 'They are not many. Good looks, an ability to wear clothes well, knowing the right people, moving in the right circles are talents that qualify us for one thing only—a wealthy marriage. A few weeks ago while we were visiting Paris, Mario almost managed to save us from bankruptcy. The daughter of a German industrialist who was staying at our hotel became infatuated with him. All seemed to be going well until one morning we came down to breakfast and discovered that she and her father had left suddenly the night before, leaving no forwarding address nor even a note of goodbye. So now,' she sighed, 'it is up to me. These diamonds are all that is left of the family fortune.

We shall sell them and take a cruise on the proceeds, hoping that one last wild gamble will result in my winning a wealthy husband. Wish me luck, Leo,' she pleaded in a husky whisper, 'wish me the same sort of luck you have had yourself.'

So sickened she felt sure she was about to vomit, Jo stumbled her way back to the powder room and, finding it empty, leant her back against the door, quivering with shocked disgust. Venetians were noted for their mercenary outlook, yet Shylock himself could be compared favourably with Leo and his friends!

Wish me the same sort of luck you have had yourself! Francesca's meaning was plain. She, too, would settle for any gullible fool with sufficient money to satisfy her craving for material possessions!

It seemed a long time before she was able to compose herself sufficiently to make her way back to the foyer, but as Mario was still not in sight it must only have been minutes. He appeared at her side just as she was considering taking flight, hailing a taxi that would transport her miles outside of Leo's vicinity. She felt she could not bear to look, much less speak to him. That he had married her for money was bad enough, but that he should discuss the situation openly with Francesca, preening himself on his good fortune, was treachery beyond belief—even for him!

Mario put her dazed look down to tiredness and was concerned. 'I'm sorry, Jo, to have kept you waiting so long, there was a queue and those damned cashiers could not have been slower! Let me help you on with your wrap; the others can't be far away. Oh, there they are ...' Mario signalled to them and they began making their way across the foyer. Jo hated Leo's spurious concern when he chided:

'Heavens, child, you look exhausted! The sooner you are in bed the better.'

Mechanically, not knowing what she said or how she said it, Jo made her goodbyes, nodding agreement with Mario's insistence that they must meet again soon and watching with frozen indifference while Francesca stood on tiptoe to kiss Leo's cheek and whisper a final word in his ear. As she sat in the car on the homeward journey, mute and deaf to his remarks, she felt his anxious glances and when he drew up outside of the villa she jumped out of the car and ran inside, paying no heed to his anxious: 'Jo, is something wrong ...?' when she sped blindly past him.

He followed her upstairs, as she suspected he would, but received no reply when after trying the locked door he called out, 'Jo, let me in! I insist upon knowing whatever it is that has upset you.'

Standing rigid by the window, she covered her ears and blanked her mind by concentrating all her attention upon a huge yellow moon coasting languidly across fathomless sky. She would not cry, she promised herself, gulping back a sob, then closed her eyes when the moon began wavering through a mist of tears.

'Jo!' Leo's voice had become dangerously calm. 'I mean to come in—must I break down the door?'

'No!' She spun from the window. 'Leave me alone, can't you? Please, just leave me in peace...'

Her broken plea seemed to have the desired effect. Footsteps moved away from the door, then there was silence. But relief was momentary. Seconds later there came a crash as his shoulder connected with a wooden panel, the flimsy lock gave way under pressure, and the door burst open. Lean, purposeful, he stepped across the threshold, pausing long enough to draw in a deep, steadying breath before condemning without anger:

'That ought not to have been necessary. Now, tell me why you are acting like a sulky child.'

Tears dried on her cheeks as she swung to face him, her slim body defiant, her expression contemptuous. 'I *was* a child—a simple innocent—but this evening I grew up! And as for my sulking— have I not the right to feel resentful, especially after overhearing your very enlightening conversation with Francesca?' Poker-stiff, she turned her back on him. 'I had become reconciled to being married for money, but obviously for you the outcome has not been satisfaction enough. Why couldn't you preen in secret instead of boasting to others about your stroke of good fortune?'

His hand descended heavily upon her shoulder. 'I haven't the faintest notion of what you are talking about.' His pretended bewilderment was infuriating. 'Exactly what is it that you are implying? So far as I can recollect there was nothing said between Francesca and myself that should cause you the least concern.' His brow wrinkled, giving an impression that he was striving to remember. 'Francesca was feeling upset, melancholy. These past few years for her have not been easy, she has had many worries——'

'The main one being how quickly she can emulate your example by finding herself a wealthy partner!' Jo spat.

His brow cleared. 'Ah, now I am beginning to understand! Francesca opened the conversation by asking why I married you and you, having been allowed to labour under certain misapprehensions, have obviously drawn the wrong conclusion from my reply. There is something which you ought to have been told sooner, Jo, information which, because of what some might term a form of conceit on my part, I deliberately withheld. But now I think the time is right to tell you——'

'More lies? No, thank you, I've heard enough!'

Her abruptness caused him to frown. He hesitated, searching her face for a hint of softening, but after thoroughly examining a defiantly tilted chin, stubborn mouth, and stormy eyes flashing green-diamond dislike, disappointment darkened his face. His lips tightened into a grim line. She knew she was being handled with kid gloves when he reached for her hand and urged quietly:

'Let us sit down and talk reasonably, Jo.'

Hating his ability to make her feel childish, she snatched her hand away. 'We have nothing to talk about!' She spun on her heel and flounced across to the window, hoping her rigid back would serve as a sign of dismissal. But the iron-willed Conte was not easily intimidated. She sensed he was mere inches away when he joined her at the window, sharing the intimacy of a darkened bedroom lit only by moonlight casting a silver veil over vibrant hair, downcast lashes and cheeks pale as the ghost she resembled as she trembled in the moonlight.

He was close enough to touch her, yet he resisted the temptation and addressed her in a calm, controlled voice. 'How are we ever to reach an understanding if we do not talk? It is wrong that so much should be left unsaid between us. Occasionally, I have hoped that we were moving towards deeper understanding—mere hours ago we were happily exploring each other's minds, enjoying each other's company, testing each other's humour and finding it sound. Can you deny, Jo, that there have been moments today when you were able to forget that on our wedding day you vowed to hate me, the man you insisted you were being forced to marry?'

Ignoring the softly phrased questions, the reminders that turned her knees to water, she seized upon the one remark that revived her anger. 'Are you daring to imply that I was *not* forced to marry you? Like my grandmother, have you foolishly concluded that deep within me are yearnings I'm too gauche to recognise?' A laugh grated past her lips. 'If that is so, then how little you know me! Let me remind you that up until our marriage I was well on my way to becoming a scientist and that for years now I've mixed with the opposite sex in an atmosphere where frank discussion of every subject—

including and especially sex—is accepted as normal, just as the liberty of women is normal and their right to have an equal say. I'm very jealous of that right, so believe me, if I were in love with you I wouldn't hesitate to say so!'

Leo thrust his hands deep into his pockets as if resisting an urge to shake her free of female arrogance. Yet his tone retained its even tenor when he vexed by her pointing out:

'Your argument would be sound were you not confusing boys with men. My own experience of English students has taught me that during their years of study they are slow to mature, full of youthful bravado yet still firmly under the family wing. Your Welfare State makes this possible by cosseting them from childhood, throwing them lifelines of grants, scholarships, and monetary aid in order that their progress through the shallows of life is made painless. Consequently, they become lazy, reluctant to strike out unaided. These boys you mistook for men no doubt treated you with sexless camaraderie. To them you were an equal—a good mate, I think you would term it—demanding no more of you than you were willing to give. They denied you your womanhood, Jo! Such a situation could never occur in my country where a boy is thrown in at the deep end of life, emerging as a man filled with the urge to master, to protect, and above all to love the woman he has chosen to be his wife.' Suddenly he closed the gap between them until he was close enough to breathe into her ear, 'Don't be afraid of the lion, *cara*, he has far more to offer than the playful puppy ...'

Mesmerised by his persuasive argument, Jo caught a sharp breath and for one unthinking moment was almost bewitched into leaning back against the shoulder looming temptingly close. Then Francesca's image flashed before her eyes, throwing a dash of sanity on to her fevered senses.

'You do well to liken yourself to a beast of the jungle,' she charged bitterly, wanting to move away but fastened by invisible chains to his side. All the applicable characteristics are yours—cunning, stealth, and a complete lack of compassion for those less ruthless than yourself.'

He recoiled from her vehemence yet kept anger from his voice when softly he reminded her, 'You did not think so this afternoon, nor again this evening when your mouth trembled as you whispered of a secret you wished me to share. What was it that you were so eager to tell me, Jo? Had you, at last, begun to recognise ... love?'

She twirled round to face him, cat-green eyes spitting fury. 'Your imagination is excelled only by your conceit, *signore*! I must admire and respect if I am to love!' Her throat closed around the word and to her utter dismay she felt tears spurting beneath her lids. Quickly she turned her head, but he had caught their glint in the moonlight. His hand snapped upwards, imprisoning her chin between forceful fingers.

Steadily, almost sadly, he noted her distress and a

flash of what could have been regret was reflected in his eyes. Painfully Jo bore his scrutiny, throat too tight to admit speech, her spirit cowed by a weight of unhappiness. She braced, expecting to have to suffer more of the tolerance she detested, but this time when he spoke his voice held a sharp edge.

'If it is any satisfaction to you, I will admit that today you have tormented me almost beyond endurance. Endlessly, I kept having to remind myself that you needed more time, that you must not be rushed. Nevertheless, there is a limit to my patience, Jo, and it is all but reached. You are young, you are innocent, but you are also my wife and I do not intend to wait for ever. I have tried—*Dio, I have tried*!'

He released her chin to run fingers through his hair, an unprecedented action for the immaculate Conte. 'I have tried to be reasonable, to make allowances for your youth and for your volatile temperament.' He bent towards her with such suddenness she was startled, alarmed by the hint of danger contained within a rock hard jaw outthrust in anger. Then to her relief temper dropped from him like a cloak as, sounding almost weary, he continued, 'More than anything in the world, little *vespa*, I wanted you to come to me of your own free will, to admit to feelings you have as yet refused to acknowledge, to be warm and soft and loving as I know you can be, as I have longed for you to be. Perhaps it is foolish of me to told on to the key that could unlock your mind of suspicion, but I wish it to be used only as a last resort. Victory will be all the sweeter if you bring me love that is strong enough to overcome doubt. I could take you now, my wife. Here, alone in this house, I could take you by force, with only the seabirds to hear your protests and the pounding waves to drown your screams.'

She recoiled from the threat, putting yards of space between them, her eyes wide with revulsion.

'Don't worry,' his tone was dry. 'I am not quite the beast you think me. I will wait a little longer, be a little more patient, and with luck the kitten might decide to purr instead of scratch.'

Nervously she edged away, sensing an extra quality in his manner, an assurance that had not been present before, a relaxed frame, a secret smile playing around his lips that seemed to indicate a certainty that sooner or later victory would be his. She stood with head bowed, a green-clad wraith bathed in moonlight that drew him like a magnet.

'Jo ...' A shudder ran through her when he reached out to clasp her lightly by the shoulder, 'why must you always fight me? I am tired of this war between us. Life could be so wonderful if only you would lay down your arms, not in defeat, but in sweet surrender.'

His magnetism was such that she did not rebel when his arm slid around her waist, drawing her close. She felt she was drowning in eyes dark with emotion yet kindling with a lick of hungry flame. '*Ti adoro*,' he murmured hoarsely. 'Come to me, *amore mio*, please ...!'

She hesitated within the circle of his arms, a tender trap held loosely so as not to frighten, offering the choice of swaying forward or jerking away.

Almost she succumbed to the bait, urged on by pounding heart-beats, by a body yearning for his touch, by a quivering mouth hungry for his kisses. He was devilish clever, a hunter with a silken snare, a lion who preferred to coax rather than to pounce.

It took overwhelming willpower to break away. Trembling, tearful, her emotions a wildly knotted tangle, she stumbled until the width of the room lay between them.

'Sorry, I can't oblige,' she choked. 'I have no intention of playing second fiddle to Francesca.'

He went very still. 'If I had wanted Francesca would I have married you?'

Her forced laughter grated shrilly through the room. 'Of course you would, so long as both she and you remain dedicated to living beyond your means! You are both misers, *signore*, and a miser's avarice entombs all other passions!'

CHAPTER THIRTEEN

WEARY of riding an emotional seesaw—one minute high with hope, the next plummeting into dejection —Jo avoided taking breakfast with Leo the next morning. Yet he sought her out, stalking easily down the path leading to the beach where he found her sorting idly through the pile of unusual seashells she had spent the previous hour collecting.

For once he did not comment upon her childish pursuits but suggested in a voice grave but nevertheless firm, 'We promised to call upon your grandmother, remember? I think today would be as good a time as any to pay her a visit.'

She started to her feet with an alacrity that was far from complimentary to her husband of just a few days. 'I should like that very much,' she agreed. 'I'll go and change.' His thoughtful eyes followed her jean-clad figure all the way, as she sped along the path leading up to the villa.

She had spent a restless night tossing and turning, wondering how she was to endure three more weeks of torment. Like a puppeteer Leo jerked the strings of her emotions first one way and then the other until she felt confused and uncertain of both her own feelings and his. One remark in particular had caused her to fret. He had implied that he was possessed of knowledge which, if confided, would cause her to revise her opinion of him. After much fruitless speculation her tired brain had rebelled and she had dismissed the remark as being yet another fabrication, an exercise in confusion evolved by a devious mind.

She dressed carefully for her visit, wanting Nònna Domini's approval, knowing that to arrive wearing trousers would be to instantly arouse her displeasure. So she chose to wear the Quaker-grey dress in which she had appeared before Leo as a penitent and was pleased with the look of demureness conjured up by a white cowl collar and spotless cuffs. To enhance this image further she brushed her hair until it glowed like silk, a banner of red, bright as courage, curling past slim, squared shoulders.

Leo made no remark about her appearance when he helped her into the boat, but as she settled into her seat she shifted uneasily, wondering if his enigmatic smile showed insight into her wish to curry favour with the grandmother whose sympathies had always seemed to err upon the side of the charming Conte.

Murano was a large island with an atmosphere very different from the rest of the Venetian communities. An island of waterborne peasants, Jo had always considered it, with its tenement blocks, lines of washing and clutter of small glass factories, grubby buildings built of red brick, with tall blackened chimneys and a wooden landing stage in front of each one.

'It is a pity,' Leo read her mind, 'that this once beautiful island should have been left to fall into such a state of disrepair. At one time Murano was considered the playground of Venice, covered with a wealth of vines and fruit trees, where aristocrats of the day kept luxurious apartments. But that was before the island was turned into a glass foundry. So many fires had erupted in Venice that all furnaces within the city were compulsorily removed to Murano, which then became the principle glass producer of Europe.'

'Is there any truth in the belief that Venetian tumblers will break into fragments if the merest drop of poison is poured into them?' she asked, a trifle shy of her lithe husband, casually dressed in light slacks and a shirt, black as his windtossed hair, with top buttons left undone baring a strong tanned throat. Sunlight glistened upon the medallion strung around his neck on a silver chain, and as he responded to her question with a grin of amusement her heart lurched, bedevilled once again by audacious charm.

'That romantic theory has many times been disproved,' he teased, amused by her obvious disappointment, 'yet knowing how tenaciously you cling to your illusions I've no doubt you'll continue believing it to be fact.'

'Can you blame me,' she countered bitterly, 'if I find illusion pleasanter than reality?'

He was still frowning when he pulled the boat in at the landing stage in front of her grandmother's house, one of a dismal terrace, its bricks grimed with the smoke from nearby factories.

'The *signora* is out visiting a friend!' called out a

neighbour leaning inquisitively from an upstair window. 'Oh, it is you, Signorina Domini!' she recognised Jo. 'Your grandmother will be back shortly, I'm certain, she is seldom absent from her home for more than an hour. Unfortunately she left a mere ten minutes ago—would you care to come inside my house and wait?'

'Thank you, no,' Jo declined hastily, 'you're very kind, but I should like to visit the factory while I'm here. Perhaps, when my grandmother returns, you would be good enough to tell her that we've arrived?'

'*Si, signorina*, that I will do.'

Almost apologetically Jo turned to Leo, whose frown had not lifted during the interchange. 'Do you mind if we visit the Renucci factory?' she enquired meekly, suspecting that a visit to a glass factory would be regarded by him as less than a novelty.

'No,' he surprised her, falling into step as she began to walk, 'it is many years since I last visited a foundry; it is time my memories of the art were revived.'

Jo had never found her grandmother's neighbours very forthcoming, but she had excused their surliness with the reminder that years of poverty and hard work could not help but result in resentment. Yet surprisingly, Leo was welcomed warmly when they entered the factory; every man present seemed intent upon shaking his hand, many calls of welcome, warm as the heat blasting from the furnaces, echoed down the long room. The owner himself appeared to greet them and to guide them around his establishment with voluble compliments and an immense amount of pride.

Jo felt piqued. For many years her grandfather had worked as *padrone di fornace* in this very factory. Diligently he had guarded the secret of the constitution of each batch, had planned the work programmes for each day, decided what items should be made and how many, had been responsible for keeping the tough craftsmen in order and when necessary had rolled up his sleeves and worked alongside them. But even this fact had not seemed to entitle her to more than a courteous nod from older workers who remembered him. Her appearance had been *tolerated*, never welcomed as it had been today.

Sensing her aggrievement, Leo explained as he introduced her to the owner, 'Signor Renucci's products were greatly favoured by the house of Tempera. Much of the glass housed within the *palazzo* was made here, exquisite, greatly admired pieces whose value has increased enormously over the years.' He turned his attention to the proprietor. 'I should like to make my wife a present, Signore Renucci, a piece of crystal of a design and purity equal to those which we treasure as heirlooms today. But first, with your permission, we will wander through the workshops before making a choice from your treasure-house.'

'It shall be my pleasure to serve you myself,' the delighted owner bowed over Jo's hand. 'Until this moment I was well pleased with the contents of my showroom, but I fear the Contessa's beauty will out-shine everything displayed upon my shelves.'

Heat from the furnace was not wholly responsible for colour rioting in Jo's cheeks as she walked by Leo's side, enduring his arm around her shoulders while he guided her through the stages of manu-facture, imparting information gained through studying the industry in depth instead of merely skimming the surface as she had herself. In spite of her embarrassment she was deeply interested, paying rapt attention to his expert commentary.

They lingered before a master glassblower hard at work beside his furnace, looking proud and self-assured, with two young apprentices handing him tools as he flourished a long pipe in his hand. Like a magician performing before an audience, he raised the pipe to his lips and puffed out his cheeks until a small bubble of glass appeared at the other end. Slanting a glance at Jo, he gave a twist of the wrist, a further delicate puff, then waved in front of her nose an as yet unidentifiable form. Swiftly he twiddled the pipe between his fingers, sliced with an iron rod, added a dollop of molten glass, then for a swift second plunged the rod into the heart of glow-ing embers. Then with a theatrical flourish he with-drew it to sever a glacial umbilical cord with a snap of iron shears. Triumphantly he placed the finished article at Jo's feet, gesturing sweating apprentices to clean up his implements in preparation for his next performance.

The swiftly-fashioned offering was simple but exquisite—a delicate, shapely bell, its ringed handle the circumference of a finger with, set alongside, a dainty crystal tear which later would be suspended from a fine chain and inserted within the bell to act as a clapper.

'To remind you of your wedding day, Contessa,' the burly glassblower bowed proudly. 'After polishing, it will be suitably boxed and presented, together with our very good wishes to yourself and the Conte, that you may enjoy a happy and fruitful marriage.'

She somehow stammered her thanks, then, with Leo grinning widely by her side, set off towards the showroom where Signor Renucci was waiting.

Leo took an interminable time deciding which of the many examples of enamelled and engraved, clear and opaque, fluted and plain, ornate and simple pieces of glass would make the most suitable present for his bride. Finally he settled for a fragile crystal goblet engraved with a frieze depicting a maned predator, unmistakably a lion, bounding in pursuit of a smaller, terrified shape which Jo sensed had appealed to his humour as being that of a timorous kitten cowering behind a flourish of foliage.

'Piteous eyes that stab the heart,' he glinted down at her, indicating his choice to the hovering proprietor. 'See how cleverly the artist has portrayed the small animal's anticipation of suffering?' Ignoring the proprietor's interest, he reached out his hand and with one taut finger levered up her chin until he was probing green, uncertain depths. 'To anticipate,' he warned softly, 'is to endure more than is necessary, *cara*.'

Her grandmother was waiting on the doorstep when they arrived back at the house. She welcomed them with a kiss, then ushered them inside, casting a questioning glance over Jo's pale face but making no comment until they were seated in the comfortable, spotlessly clean living-room. Not until coffee had been poured and a plateful of small biscuits passed around did her grandmother settle back in her chair to chide Leo lightly, 'I had expected to see my granddaughter blooming, *signore*, instead of which she is sad and pale as a chaste little nun.'

Colour flared in Jo's cheeks. Her grandmother was impossible to deceive; her eyes grew shrewder, her tongue more cutting with age.

Leo, however, refused to be embarrassed. Casting a negligent eye over Jo, a picture of confusion in her grey dress with Quaker-prim collar and cuffs, he observed lightly, 'You must know that Jo is a creature of contrasting moods, one day outrageous, the next demure. Today she has opted to be the subdued young penitent—why, I am not quite sure, but I do not complain. It is not every man who can awaken each day to a new and different wife. I must confess I find the experience both challenging and intriguing.'

Nònna Domini looked pleased. 'Good,' she leant forward to pat his hand. 'Jo takes more understanding than most, needs firmer discipline than most, but I can see that she is in sympathetic hands. Now,' she sat upright and beamed at them both, 'I have some good news for you! Sara and Vincente have set a date for their wedding. It is to take place next week. Your father, Jo, demurred at first, he wanted them to wait at least until you and Leo had returned from your honeymoon, but after pressure was brought to bear, he was finally persuaded that a one-day interruption would not be too upsetting for you both. He stipulated, however, that you were not to be told until the very last minute. A message was to have been sent the day before the wedding summoning you both to attend.

'Happily, your arrival here today has made that unnecessary. All arrangements have been made, invitations sent out, and preparations for the wedding feast are well under way. It is exciting, is it not?' she appealed, bird-bright, 'having two weddings in the family within the space of a month? I suspect, Jo, that your father is feeling relieved as well as pleased —the responsibility of controlling two wayward daughters was becoming a great strain. You too, *signore*,' she addressed Leo, 'must be pleased that your cousin's future has been decided. Sisters married to cousins is a very tidy arrangement, I think. So beneficial that the outcome might almost have been planned.'

Beneficial! The benefit was all on one side, Jo fumed. Both Leo and Vincente had been up for sale and her father had considered them a good investment!

So moody and withdrawn did she become that when the time came for them to leave her grandmother drew her to one side, showing obvious impatience. 'I don't know what to make of you today, Jo! Your manner has been most ungracious, especially towards the attentive and very charming Conte. I am beginning to suspect that you have been spoiled, child. Can't you show a little more gratitude towards your husband?'

Gratitude for what? Jo fumed inwardly, at the same time managing somehow to smile. Gratitude that her father had been rich enough to meet the Conte's price?

When Leo swung the boat in a wide arc, starting upon the return journey to the wild and lonely shore, she felt she was a prisoner being deported into exile. Steeped in depression, she sat silent, her demure expression hiding a mind in turmoil as she explored every avenue of thought directed towards a solution to a situation that was becoming more unbearable by the minute. Her grandmother's news had practically effected her release. With the arrangements for Sara's wedding so well advanced her her father's hands were virtually tied, for to cancel the wedding at such a late stage would be to inflict cruel unhappiness upon Sara and humiliation upon the Tempera pride. Therefore, she reasoned, escape was now possible. The only problem remaining was how!

When Leo attempted to help her along the path leading to the villa she jerked away, loathing his touch. That her revulsion had been communicated was obvious by his tone when he halted her progress through the shrubbery with the clipped, icy observation:

'I am fast reaching the conclusion that my handling of you has been all wrong. Patience, I thought, was all that was needed. I told myself that once removed from her father's indulgence the child would develop quickly into a woman. But as the days have passed and you have grown progressively more wilful, more prone to moods, I have been finding it very difficult to control an impulse to turn you across my knee and administer a good spanking!'

With unusual roughness he pulled her towards him, eyes glittering coldly as they travelled her defiant face, daring her to rebel. 'Well, which do you prefer—slaps or kisses?' It sounded like an ultimatum! 'This situation has remained tolerable because only we two were aware that it existed. But very shortly our seclusion is to end and we will be once more surrounded by family and inquisitive friends. I utterly refuse,' he clamped, tightening his grip upon her arm, 'to be the recipient of any further remarks similar to those voiced by your very observant grandmother.'

His black head swooped until his lips were a fraction from hers. 'The old lady was correct,' he murmured, softly threatening, 'you do have the look of a chaste, untouched nun. It will be my enjoyable duty to remedy that. By the time we leave this island I promise you, *cara*, that everyone who wonders shall have his curiosity satisfied. One glance at your expressive face will be sufficient to confirm that you have experienced the sweet tempestuous passion that is the reward of every dutiful young bride!'

'You should be so lucky!' Panic caused her to revert to the vernacular favoured student friends whose attitude towards authority had always been brusque. She jerked away and began running towards the villa, not stopping until she had gained the safety of her bedroom where she leant her back against a door rendered useless as a barricade because of a shattered lock. But he did not follow her. For almost half an hour she waited, tense body pressed hard against the door, before gradually she was able to relax.

'Well, Jo,' she muttered to herself as she paced the room, 'it's now or never—those were not idle threats, he meant every word. Which follows that you must leave here tonight at the very latest!' She paced and pondered until she was weary, latching eagerly on to one escape plan after another, then discarding each as hopeless. If she were to try to escape by car the sound of the engine would bring him running, even if she were fortunate enough to find out where he kept the keys. To walk to the Lido and then catch a waterbus to Venice was out of the question; she would be missed and followed long before she had reached the town. She thought of asking Dina to help, then dismissed this as placing an unfair burden upon the conscience of the girl who, though sympathetic, would nevertheless feel she must remain loyal to her employer.

Then with a flash of inspiration she remembered

the haste with which Leo had followed her from the landing stage. Was it possible, had his anger been consuming enough to have caused him to forget to remove the ignition key from the motorboat? The more she thought the more convinced she became that he had. Unfortunately it was too dangerous to check; the sight of her slipping down to the landing stage might serve as a reminder, and she dared not risk that. She would have to act very carefully; her attitude during dinner must be sufficiently disarming to make him think escape was the last thing on her mind, then, once the meal was over and darkness could provide cover, she must think up an excuse to leave him for a while. If her acting were convincing enough, and his suspicions lulled, she should be halfway across the lagoon before he began wondering about the length of her absence.

She took great pains with her appearance. The dress she wore for dinner had to be flattering enough to disarm him, yet must not hamper her progress when she ran down to the beach. Her final choice was a widely-flaring evening skirt, chestnut brown with matching sequined jacket, but with tight, full-length sleeves that would protect her arms from the evening breeze. Swiftness would be the essence of her escape. There would not be time even to grab a wrap, so bearing this in mind she slid a long chiffon scarf through the bracelet on her wrist. Its protection would be flimsy, but at least it would turn a little of the chill from her exposed neckline. She felt proud and rather clever as she twirled before a mirror, then began pacing, nervous as an actress awaiting her cue.

The ordeal began immediately Leo pushed open the door and strode into her bedroom. He was handsome enough to play the part of any woman's hero, she admitted grudgingly, avoiding eyes that raked approval over her body, bold, unrepentant eyes showing a glint of ... *anticipation*?

Inwardly shivering, she forced herself to smile and move towards him. Looking pleased, he admitted dryly, 'I half expected to find you sulking—either that or dressed in the most objectionable manner in the hope of cooling my ardour. But, as usual, you have surprised me by appearing quite enchanting. Can it be that once again I have misjudged you? Have you suddenly become mature and wise enough to accept without a fight that which you sense is inevitable?'

She cringed against the need for diplomacy. Curbing a feline urge to scratch and spit, she schooled herself to purr, 'To argue against the inevitable is a waste of time. Rather than rail against a storm I put on a raincoat.'

His golden eyes glowed. Halting her progress towards the door, he clasped both her hands in his and turned her round to face him. Softly, with a pleased smile playing around his lips, he asked, 'Is this your way of admitting surrender, Jo?'

'Perhaps,' she choked through a throat agonisingly tight, wishing for one reckless moment that the lie were truth. 'Give me a little more time, Leo,' she stammered, then hoodwinked him completely when with a small breathless laugh, she admitted, 'You'll probably think me foolish, but I'm ... I'm feeling rather shy.'

She had never felt more ashamed when, with protective tenderness, he tucked her hand into the crook of his elbow and began escorting her downstairs.

CHAPTER FOURTEEN

As dinner progressed Jo was astonished at the extent of Leo's blindness to the trap she had prepared, at his eagerness to swallow her bait. They ate by candlelight, speaking little as each course progressed, Jo because she was too busy trying not to cry and Leo because he had no wish to rush the victory she had hinted was imminent, content to bide his time until the meal was over and Dina had gone home, leaving them to their solitude.

But once or twice their fingers touched, the small contact causing her simultaneous pangs of fear and delight. She sensed his eyes upon her downbent head but would not look up. She must be performing well, she congratulated herself, or he would not be sitting opposite looking benign as a well fed jungle cat, his golden eyes slumbrous, yet ready at his partner's whim to join her in play. Nervously she laid down her fork. To stroke a lion took nerve enough —from where would she find courage to inflict a wound?

When the meal was finished Dina served coffee, then cleared away. Not long afterwards she popped her head around the door to beam, 'With your permission, *signore, signora*, I will go now. Unless there is anything else you wish ...?'

'Nothing, thank you.' Leo's obvious desire to be

left alone with his lovely wife delighted Dina. *'Buona notte,'* he dismissed her firmly, 'we'll see you tomorrow.'

Dina's exit signalled the end of the prologue—now it was time to continue with the play!

'Shall we move into the *salotto* where it is more comfortable?' he suggested. Jo implied agreement by rising to her feet, then she hesitated, eyes widening as if at some sudden reminder. 'Oh, how careless of me! All during dinner some small doubt has been nagging at the back of my mind, and now I've realised why! Just before you came into my room I lit a cigarette and for the life of me I can't remember stubbing it out. Would you excuse me while I slip upstairs and check?'

'Don't bother, I'll go . . .' Leo offered, but she had almost reached the door.

'No,' she insisted, 'I won't be more than a few minutes.'

Hastily she closed the door behind her, then ran hell for leather to the back entrance, through the garden, then along the path, blessing her foresight in choosing to wear serviceable sandals instead of the spike-heeled, fragile bundle of straps she usually favoured. Without sparing time to even glance across her shoulder she sped onwards, her brown-clad figure almost invisible in the darkness. When at last she reached the boat she tumbled into it, groping feverishly in the darkness for the feel of the vital key without which the engine would not start. For five minutes she groped, sobbing with her anxiety, unwilling to accept that no key had been left for her to find, then she slumped against a seat shivering with the cold of despair.

'Hypocrite, thy name is woman—Josephine Tempera, to be precise!' The bitter accusation scythed through the darkness. 'I congratulate you, *bella*, for acting out your lie with astonishing sincerity!'

His words pierced her shell of despair, sending heat racing through her veins as fiery temper erupted. Jumping from the boat, she quivered in front of him.

'You dare to call me a hypocrite! *You*, who did not hesitate to marry me while carrying on an affair with Francesca—*you*, who spoke of wanting a loving wife, a mother for your children, when, as everyone in Venice is aware, what you really wanted was a share of my father's wealth!'

Golden eyes glittered in the darkness, chilling, intent, menacing as those of a jungle cat who has been prodded and aggravated beyond endurance. Sensing within him a violence never before encountered, Jo began backing away, but had taken no more than a step when the predator pounced. Ferocious fingers clawed into her shoulders as he jerked her forward and proceeded to shake her violently until her teeth chattered and her head felt as if it were about to snap from her body, at the same time clipping words through tightly compressed lips. 'Wild, wilful shrew! This time you have tried me too far, I am determined you shall be tamed!'

Fear came to her aid, fear of the ferocious stranger who had taken the place of the even-tempered, hard-to-rile Conte who had brushed aside her insults and smiled indulgence of her childish whims. With all the spirit of a firebrand kitten she tried to wriggle out of his clutches and when her efforts met with no success resorted to the ultimate feline defence of raking vicious fingernails down the length of his cheek.

'*Diavolo!*' Instinctively he lifted his hand to the scratches and the second her shoulder was released Jo wrenched away and fled into the darkness.

Thorns stabbed through her long skirt, impeding her progress as she stumbled through undergrowth, over rocks and boulders, then finally on to a firm stretch of sand. Gulping in a couple of sharp, painful breaths, she picked up her tattered skirts and ran blindly, neither knowing or caring where her flight would end, anxious only to put as much distance as possible between herself and the man whose footsteps she could hear pounding in her wake. Terror fluttered inside of her like the wings of a frantic bird when she stumbled and fell, losing precious minutes in the race. Her terrified senses assured her that Leo was quickly making ground; even as she scrambled to her feet she imagined she could feel the heat of his breath searing the nape of her neck.

She screamed aloud when an impact behind the knees sent her sprawling face downward upon the sand. Rough hands rolled her on to her back and for seconds, too winded to speak, she had to be content with glaring indignant defiance into his unrepentant face.

'Beast!' She choked on a mouthful of sand. 'You took an unfair advantage—rugby tackles belong on a rugby field!'

'Just as honeyed responses belong on the lips of a woman who intends to honour her promises,' he countered tersely, pressing the weight of his body on her legs and grasping each of her wrists so that she was effectively pinned to the ground. 'Now, you will listen to what I have to say!'

She shuddered from the breathed threat but was too tightly held to offer physical resistance. 'Talk all night, if you like,' she retorted bitterly, 'I shall simply refuse to believe a word you say.'

Exercising the utmost control, he ignored her taunt and proceeded in tight, clipped tones. 'First of all, let us dispose of the least important matter— namely Francesca. She and I have been friends since childhood, that perhaps has made her feel she is entitled to show a proprietorial interest in my doings, I don't know—all I do know is that there has never been the slightest romantic attachment between us.'

Inside of her, frantic wings ceased flapping and went very still. 'Knowing what a minx she can be, I should have thought to warn you of her liking for drama and of her unfortunate tendency towards making innuendoes that are completely devoid of truth, but to be honest, these past few weeks Francesca has been the very last person on my mind. However, now that she has accepted our marriage as fact, you will probably discover that she can be a very good friend, loyal, partisan to a fault, and genuinely delighted—in her ignorance—that we have found happiness together. Her request, "Wish me the same sort of luck you have had yourself", was influenced by thoughts of love and not, as you suspected, by thoughts of money.'

When Jo uttered a derogatory 'Huh!' he winced, but continued bleakly, 'Now that small item has been disposed of I can deal with the matter that has caused you most concern—namely that of finance. I had hoped to explain in more favourable circumstances, had even been foolish enough to hope,' his lips twisted wryly, 'that after getting to know me better you would have no doubts left to erase. But as you are still so obviously bigoted against me, so unresponsive to reason, I think the time has come to tell you that far from being a pauper, I could match, lira for lira, the total amount of your father's wealth.'

Sand-encrusted lashes flew up over green eyes brilliant with disbelief. 'You must consider me every kind of a fool if you expect me to believe that!' she spat contemptuously.

His patrician features hardened; obviously the Conte was not accustomed to being accused of lying. 'Proof can be supplied if and whenever it should be needed,' he replied, flaring nostrils indicating his distaste of the whole subject.

'My father would have mentioned——' she began.

'Your father was requested by me to avoid the subject,' he cut in. 'For reasons already stated, I did not wish you to know. However, I will free him of his promise so that when you ask him—or anyone else you might care to question—he will tell you that far from being the dilettante you think me I have for many years worked upon the restoration of my city's ancient buildings. During the course of such work I have acquired not only a reputation as an expert but also an embarrassing amount of the commodity upon which you set such great store: money. I did not seek such wealth, my main consideration was the preservation of irreplaceable buildings for the benefit of future generations. Towards such an end I would gladly have worked for nothing.'

Jo closed her ears against the sincerity in his voice, reluctant to believe that she could have so badly misjudged him, *refusing* to believe it. Suffering his piercing look, she relaxed, twisted her lips into the semblance of a smile and enquired, sweetly mocking, 'Do you have any more fairy tales to tell me? If not, I should like to be released so that I can return to the villa.'

For what seemed a very long time Leo stared down at her, golden eyes dark with anger. A huge moon sailed from behind cloud, bathing in its silver glow the girl outstretched upon the sand in the attitude of an offering awaiting sacrifice. The sight seemed to incense him, the glitter she feared appearing once more to terrorise her as slowly his black head lowered towards lips whose tilt of bravado was denied by a quiver of dismay.

'But I have not finished with you yet, *amore mio*.' She blanched from the softly growled threat. 'Did you not hear me promise that before we left the island the shrew would be tamed?' When he kissed her it was as if her bones melted into the sand, leaving behind a weak, helpless body completely at the mercy of hands that blazed a trail of fire along a smooth line of shoulder, a curve of breast, a slender hollowed waist, then lingered against a length of thigh. He laughed softly against her lips, revelling in his dominance, satisfied that he held her spellbound.

That small laugh of triumph was his undoing, the whip that flogged awake her pride and drove a stab of cunning through her numbed mind.

'Leo ...!' Instilling melting tenderness into her voice, she snuggled against him. 'Darling, what a fool I've been ...' He drew a pleased breath, then when his imprisoning arms relaxed into a loving embrace she whispered messages of remorse into his ear, at the same time furtively stretching a hand behind his back, groping for a weapon of defence among the sand. She almost gasped her relief when her fingers closed around a large stone. Giving herself no time to think, she grabbed it and thrust it with all her might against the back of his downbent head. The thud as it connected was sickening. Panic-stricken, she clawed her way from under him when he slumped senseless, then again she fled, this time in the direction of the villa.

Great gasping sobs escaped her as she forced herself not to look back, not to think about the unconscious body laid out defenceless on the beach. She had to reach the car before he came round; this was her last chance of escape from a now desperate situation and she dared not allow it to slip through her fingers.

Tears were streaming down her cheeks when she stumbled into the villa, then raced upstairs to Leo's bedroom where she hoped to find the car keys. She was shaking so much she could barely turn the door-knob, but after a deep breath to steady her nerves she thrust open the door and ran inside. The room was bare, monastic even, but as she ran across to the dressing-table his presence was so strong it felt almost physical.

A faint tang of aftershave was emanating from behind a half-open door leading into the bathroom, the aroma of a recently-smoked cheroot teased her nostrils, a bathrobe flung across the bed brought vividly to mind the inert body stretched out on the sand, and as her shaking fingers searched through the articles on top of the dressing-table they brushed against a gold cufflink, upturning it so that her eye was caught by the baleful glare of a monogrammed lion. Swiftly she jerked her hand away and ran across to a wardrobe, sliding open the door in search of the jacket Leo had worn when last he had garaged the car. It seemed an unforgivable intrusion to rummage through the pockets of immaculate suits, but she forced herself to do it, searching feverishly, conscious that at any moment he might appear in the doorway bitter, angry, and thirsting for revenge.

When at last her fingers closed around a bunch of keys her relief was so enormous she sagged against the wall until she had mustered sufficient strength to resume her flight. She blessed her good luck when, after negotiating the stairs and hall without incident, she ran outside to the garage. Clouds had dispersed and a full moon was throwing sufficient light to make the unlocking of the garage doors easy. Seconds later Jo was nosing the powerful sports car out of the garage, her shaking body crouched over a wheel held in tense fingers. She had managed to outwit the athletic Conte who in the past had outrun, outwalked and outswum her at every opportunity!

Then almost without volition her foot stamped hard upon the brake pedal. Why was Leo not in hot pursuit? It was against his nature to admit defeat, so what possible reason could there be behind his non-appearance?

The nose of the car was jutting out into the roadway leading to the Lido, a mere half hour's drive away, yet she switched off the engine, pulled on the handbrake and stared wide-eyed through the windscreen as a dreadful thought struck her. Could the blow she had struck have killed him? Was he lying on the beach felled by a mortal blow from a stone directed by her own reckless hand?

'Oh, no ...!' she moaned, covering her face with shaking hands. 'Please, God, no ...!'

She could not afterwards recall her journey back to the beach, but stamped indelibly upon her mind was the sight of Leo's prostrate body lying immobile on the sand where she had left him. Incoherent prayers were interspersed with agonised gasps as she stumbled down the path and ran to drop on to her knees beside him.

'Leo! Leo, my darling,' she sobbed, 'please speak to me—don't die, I couldn't bear it if you should die!' She had no idea what she said or promised during the five long minutes while she rolled him on his back, brushed sand from his hair and forehead and began stroking his cheeks with frantic fingers. 'Leo,' she choked. 'My darling, I love you so much!'

Dredging her memory for hints on first aid, she slipped her hand inside his jacket to search for a heartbeat and felt a steady, comforting throb beneath her palm. Immeasurably relieved, she strove for further reminders and recalling instructions on how to administer the kiss of life she propped herself up with one hand on either side of his head and lowered her mouth towards his.

The moment their lips touched he came alive— vitally, excitingly alive—with arms that crushed her close and warm, passionate lips that murmured hoarse, adoring condemnation as he rolled her back against the sand and proceeded to punish her in the most wonderful way possible for all the heartache, frustration and pain she had inflicted during the past traumatic weeks.

Surprised, breathless, and utterly confused, Jo nevertheless realised that she had been tricked. Yet the delight of knowing him to be alive overruled every other thought in those first few startling seconds. The agony of mind she had endured when she had thought him dead, the idea of living her life without his teasing, his tormenting and above all his tenderness had almost caused her own heart to stop beating. Those moments had convinced her that her career, her freedom, even the heartache of being married for reasons other than love did not matter, all she wanted was the feel of his arms around her, his kisses upon her lips, and to hear the meltingly tender expressions of love which at that very moment were being whispered into her ear.

'*Io ti amo, mia cara!* Oh, *tesoro mio,*' he groaned, burying his lips in her bright hair, 'I had almost given up hope. Tell me again what you told me when you thought I could not hear,' he pleaded urgently. 'Look at me with your honest eyes and let me see the truth reflected there when you speak.'

Jo did not pretend. Sliding her arms across his broad shoulders, feeling muscles flex beneath her touch, she admitted in a small, broken whisper, 'Leo, my own darling, I adore you so much I couldn't bear the thought of living without you ...'

Never had the reward for surrender been so sweet. Gathering her into his arms as if she were infinitely precious, infinitely fragile, he sought her lips, drawing the heart from her body with a kiss achingly tender, a kiss that pledged a lifetime of devotion and set a seal upon her heart, marking her for ever with the stamp of the possessive Temperas.

There were no stars in the sky brighter than her eyes when, suppressing the tide of passion rising within him, he pulled her to her feet, concerned as ever for her wellbeing. 'Come, *cara*, let us return to the villa.'

'But why ...?' She stretched out her arms as if to embrace all about her, enchanted by the beauty of the night, by the silver moon with its huge benevolent smile that seemed to be lingering on its pathway through the heavens to enjoy the sight of their happiness, by the soft murmur of waves upon the shore sighing a song of envy, by the warm bed of sand that had enclosed them within its warm embrace.

'Because,' he shook her gently, a tolerant smile playing around his mouth, 'though you may perhaps not have noticed, my darling, the breeze is growing colder. And besides that,' he drew her close to nuzzle into the warm hollow of her throat, 'in years to come when we are recalling our wedding night, I do not wish you to be able to rebuke me for having spent it on a cold, comfortless beach.'

He felt the quiver that ran through her and tightened his arm, holding her very still. 'Are you afraid of me, Jo?' he asked quietly.

To his relief she nestled closer to his heart and assured him with a contented sigh, 'Never of you, Leo.'

He hugged her so that she felt cosseted as a child wrapped in a cloak of love and rocked her slightly as he promised, 'I shall be gentle, Jo. Trust me ...?'

'Always.' She reached up to stroke his cheek as if he and not she were in need of reassurance. 'Always and completely, my darling.'

They savoured the short journey back to the villa, strolling along the path they knew would lead them to paradise, yet lingering every now and then to kiss, to caress and to talk, dispersing every last doubt. Gazing across the sea to where the lights of Venice were glittering in the darkness, Jo spoke in a wondering murmur. 'Had I not turned back because I was worried about you I would be in Venice now. You tricked me by pretending to be unconscious,' she reproved him. 'I suffered agonies thinking you might be dead.'

'Good,' he teased, squeezing hard where his hand rested on the curve of her waist, 'you deserve to share a little of the suffering I have endured on your account.' He then amended his severity with a kiss before continuing in a more serious vein, 'After you hit me I was stunned for a few seconds, and when I had shaken off my daze my first impulse was to follow you, intending first of all to dump you in the sea and then alleviate my anger by administering a thorough spanking.'

'You wouldn't have ...!' She rounded on him indignantly.

'I assure you, my darling, that I would,' he replied, controlling quirking lips with difficulty. 'However, upon reflection, I decided that if you were able to leave me—as you thought, unconscious —then obviously there was no chance of your ever loving me and the dream I had cherished from our first moment of meeting would have to be discarded, I would have to accept, finally and irrevocably, that you were not the girl for me.'

Halfway towards the villa he stopped to cup her small, serious face between his palms. 'Thank God you did come back, Jo! As I lay there on the beach listening to the revving of the car that was taking you away from me I descended into hell and believed I would never surface. Then you came running, sobbing your fears for my life, and it suddenly seemed that agony had served to intensify joy.'

After a kiss to ascertain that she was real and not a mirage, Jo betrayed her uncertainty by latching on to one particular remark. 'You said,' she swallowed hard, 'the dream you had cherished from our first moment of meeting ...?'

'You sound as if you find that hard to believe,' he reproved her gently.

'How can I believe it,' she continued, desperately wanting to be convinced, 'when I first appeared before you dressed in the most hideous garments I could find, with a mask of paint covering my face that wouldn't have disgraced a clown.'

'That made no difference,' he assured her with such sincerity her heart soared. 'I must admit that when you appeared, defiant and outrageous, in front of my easily shocked relatives, my first impulse was to laugh. Then I saw behind the façade, recognised courage, and realised that beneath the mask of paint the little clown was crying.'

'Oh, Leo,' she crumpled against him, 'how tolerant you are—and how well you know me.'

'You are part of me, my heart,' he told her simply, 'with you I hear one word and understand two. My only regret is that we have wasted so much time.'

He stooped to lift her into his arms as the outline of the villa loomed before them. 'I am greedy for you, little wife. If life were as permanent as the shadows cast by mountains I would not worry, but as it can be compared with the shadow of a fish skimming through water every precious moment must be savoured.'

Impatiently, he kicked open the door of the villa and carried her over the threshold. For a time there was movement and laughter inside, then one by one lights were extinguished and only a broadly smiling moon was permitted to share the secrets of the silent villa.

Send coupon today for
FREE
Harlequin Presents
Catalog

We'll send you by return mail a complete listing
of all the wonderful Harlequin Presents novels
still in stock.

Here's your chance to catch up on all the
delightful reading you may have missed
because the books are no longer available at
your favorite booksellers.

Fill in this handy order form and mail it today.

Harlequin Reissues

Harlequin Reissues

Complete and mail this coupon today!

Harlequin Reader Service
MPO Box 707
Niagara Falls, N.Y. 14302·

In Canada:
649 Ontario St.
Stratford, Ont. N5A 6W2

Please send me the following Harlequin Romances. I am enclosing my check or money order for 95¢ for each novel ordered, plus 25¢ to cover postage and handling.

☐ 1282	☐ 1394	☐ 1481
☐ 1284	☐ 1397	☐ 1483
☐ 1285	☐ 1433	☐ 1484
☐ 1288	☐ 1435	☐ 1638
☐ 1289	☐ 1439	☐ 1643
☐ 1292	☐ 1440	☐ 1647
☐ 1293	☐ 1444	☐ 1651
☐ 1294	☐ 1449	☐ 1652
☐ 1295	☐ 1456	☐ 1654
☐ 1353	☐ 1457	☐ 1659
☐ 1363	☐ 1462	☐ 1675
☐ 1365	☐ 1464	☐ 1677
☐ 1368	☐ 1468	☐ 1686
☐ 1371	☐ 1473	☐ 1691
☐ 1372	☐ 1475	☐ 1695
☐ 1384	☐ 1477	☐ 1697
☐ 1390	☐ 1478	

Number of novels checked _____ @ 95¢ each = $_____

N.Y. and N.J. residents add appropriate sales tax $_____

Postage and handling $_____.25

                              TOTAL $_____

NAME _____
                    (Please print)

ADDRESS _____

CITY _____

STATE/PROV. _____ ZIP/POSTAL CODE _____

ROM 2152